John Ford's The Broken Heart: A Retelling

David Bruce

Published by David Bruce, 2022.

Table of Contents

Dedication

Dedicated to Carl Eugene Bruce and Josephine Saturday Bruce

My father, Carl Eugene Bruce, died on 24 October 2013. He used to work for Ohio Power, and at one time, his job was to shut off the electricity of people who had not paid their bills. He sometimes would find a home with an impoverished mother and some children. Instead of shutting off their electricity, he would tell the mother that she needed to pay her bill or soon her electricity would be shut off. He would write on a form that no one was home when he stopped by because if no one was home he did not have to shut off their electricity.

The best good deed that anyone ever did for my father occurred after a storm that knocked down many power lines. He and other linemen worked long hours and got wet and cold. Their feet were freezing because water got into their boots and soaked their socks. Fortunately, a kind woman gave my father and the other linemen dry socks to wear.

My mother, Josephine Saturday Bruce, died on 14 June 2003. She used to work at a store that sold clothing. One day, an impoverished mother with a baby clothed in rags walked into the store and started shoplifting in an interesting way: The mother took the rags off her baby and dressed the infant in new clothing. My mother knew that this mother could not afford to buy the clothing, but she helped the mother dress her baby and then she watched as the mother walked out of the store without paying.

***

The doing of good deeds is important. As a free person, you can choose to live your life as a good person or as a bad person. To be a good person, do good deeds. To be a bad person, do bad deeds. If you do good deeds, you will become good. If you do bad deeds, you will become bad. To become the person you want to be, act as if you already are that kind of person. Each of us chooses what kind of person we will become. To become a good person, do the things a good person does. To become a bad person, do the things a bad person does. The opportunity to take action to become the kind of person you want to be is yours.

Human beings have free will. According to the Babylonian Niddah 16b, whenever a baby is to be conceived, the Lailah (angel in charge of contraception) takes the drop of semen that will result in the conception and asks God, "Sovereign of the Universe, what is going to be the fate of this drop? Will it develop into a robust or into a weak person? An intelligent or a stupid person? A wealthy or a poor person?" The Lailah asks all these questions, but it does not ask, "Will it develop into a righteous or a wicked person?" The answer to that question lies in the decisions to be freely made by the human being that is the result of the conception.

A Buddhist monk visiting a class wrote this on the chalkboard: "EVERYONE WANTS TO SAVE THE WORLD, BUT NO ONE WANTS TO HELP MOM DO THE DISHES." The students laughed, but the monk then said, "Statistically, it's highly unlikely that any of you will ever have the opportunity to run into a burning orphanage and rescue an infant. But, in the smallest gesture of kindness — a warm smile, holding the door for the person behind you, shoveling the driveway of the elderly person next door — you have committed an act of immeasurable profundity, because to each of us, our life is our universe."

In her book titled *I Have Chosen to Stay and Fight*, comedian Margaret Cho writes, "I believe that we get complimentary snack-size portions of the afterlife, and we all receive them in a different way." For Ms. Cho, many of her snack-size portions of the afterlife come in hip hop music. Other people get different snack-size portions of the afterlife, and we all must be on the lookout for them when they come our way. And perhaps doing good deeds and experiencing good deeds are snack-size portions of the afterlife.

The Zen master Gisan was taking a bath. The water was too hot, so he asked a student to add some cold water to the bath. The student brought a bucket of cold water, added some cold water to the bath, and then threw the rest of the water on a rocky path. Gisan scolded the student: "Everything can be used. Why did you waste the rest of the water by pouring it on the path? There are some plants nearby which could have used the water. What right do you have to waste even a drop of water?" The student became enlightened and changed his name to Tekisui, which means "Drop of Water."

Educate Yourself
Read Like A Wolf Eats
Be Excellent to Each Other
Books Then, Books Now, Books Forever

***

In this retelling, as in all my retellings, I have tried to make the work of literature accessible to modern readers who may lack the knowledge about mythology, religion, and history that the literary work's contemporary audience had.

Do you know a language other than English? If you do, I give you permission to translate this book, copyright your translation, publish or self-publish it, and keep all the royalties for yourself. (Do give me credit, of course, for the original retelling.)

I would like to see my retellings of classic literature used in schools, so I give permission to the country of Finland (and all other countries) to give copies of this book to all students forever. I also give permission to the state of Texas (and all other states) to give copies of this book to all students forever. I also give permission to all teachers to give copies of this book to all students forever.

Teachers need not actually teach my retellings. Teachers are welcome to give students copies of my eBooks as background material. For example, if they are teaching Homer's *Iliad* and *Odyssey*, teachers are welcome to give students copies of my *Virgil's* Aeneid: *A Retelling in Prose* and tell students, "Here's another ancient epic you may want to read in your spare time."

CAST OF CHARACTERS
The Speakers' Names Fitted to their Qualities

Amelus: *Trusty*, young Friend to Nearchus, Prince of Argos.

Amyclas: *Historical name common to the Kings of Laconia*. King of Sparta.

Armostes: *an Appeaser*, a Counselor of State. Uncle to Ithocles and Penthea.

Bassanes: *Vexation*, a jealous Nobleman. Husband to Penthea. He is a wealthy older man.

Calantha: *Flower of beauty*, King Amyclas' Daughter. Later engaged to Ithocles. Heiress to the throne of Sparta.

Chrystalla: *Crystal*, Female attendant to Calantha.

Crotolon: *Noise*, another Counselor of State. Father of Orgilus.

Euphrania: *Joy*, Female attendant to Calantha, and Daughter to Crotolon. Sister of Orgilus. Later wife to Bassanes.

Grausis: *Old Beldam*, Overseer/attendant of Penthea. She is an old lady. A beldam is an evil old woman.

Groneas: *Tavern-haunter*, a Courtier.

Hemophil: *Glutton*, a Courtier.

Ithocles: *Honor of loveliness*, a Favorite. Twin brother of Penthea. General of King Amyclas' army. He is a young man.

Nearchus: *Young Prince*, Prince of Argos. Cousin and suitor to Calantha.

Orgilus: *Angry*, son to Crotolon. Formerly engaged to Penthea. Disguised for a while as a scholar named Aplotes (quality: simplicity).

Penthea: *Complaint*, Sister to Ithocles. Wife to Bassanes. Formerly engaged to Orgilus. She is a young woman.

Philema: *A Kiss*, Female attendant to Calantha.

Phulas: *Watchful*, Servant to Bassanes.

Prophilus: *Dear*, Friend to Ithocles. Later husband to Euphrania.

Tecnicus: *Artist*, a Philosopher. Advisor to Orgilus. He can interpret the Delphic Oracle.

Lords, Courtiers, Officers, Attendants, etc.

Other Persons

Thrasus: *Fierceness*, Father of Ithocles. (Already dead.)
Aplotes: *Simplicity*, Orgilus so disguised.

***

SCENE— *Sparta.*
Sparta is located in Laconia, aka Lacedaemon, in Greece.

CHAPTER 1

— 1.1 —

Crotolon and Orgilus talked together in a room in Crotolon's house. Crotolon was a counselor of state, and Orgilus was his son. The two men were arguing.

"Trifle with me no longer," Crotolon said. "I will know the reason that makes you hasten to take this journey."

"My reason!" Orgilus said. "Good sir, I can give you many reasons."

"Give me one reason, a good one," Crotolon said. "Such a reason I expect, and before we part I must have one.

"Athens! Please, why do you want to go to Athens? You do not intend to kick against the world and become a Cynic or Stoic philosopher."

Cynic philosophers contemptuously rejected wealth and pleasure. Stoic philosophers accepted and endured suffering, and they had strict ethical standards.

Crotolon continued, "Nor do you intend to study logic, or become an Areopagite — a member of the Areopagus, the highest judicial court in Athens — and be a judge in cases concerning the commonwealth, for, as I take it, the budding of your chin cannot prognosticate so grave an honor. To be a member of the Areopagus, you should have a long beard."

"All this I acknowledge," Orgilus said.

"You do!" Crotolon said. "Then, son, if books and love of knowledge inflame you to undertake this travel, here in Sparta you may as freely study."

"That is not what I meant, sir," Orgilus said. "I meant that all this that you have said is true. I do not want what you mentioned, sir. Not that, sir."

"Not that, sir!" Crotolon said. "As your father, I command you to acquaint me with the truth."

"Thus I obey you," Orgilus replied. "After so many quarrels as dissension, fury, and rage had pierced in blood, and sometimes with death to such confederates as sided with now-dead Thrasus — the father of Ithocles — and to those who sided with yourself, my lord, our present Spartan king, Amyclas, reconciled your eager, bitter swords and sealed a gentle peace.

"You and Thrasus professed yourselves to be friends, and to confirm this friendship, a resolution for a lasting league between your families was entertained by joining in a Hymeneal — marriage — bond me and the fair Penthea, the only daughter of Thrasus."

"What about this?" Crotolon asked.

"It is important by much, much, dear sir," Orgilus said. "A freedom of converse, an interchange of holy and chaste love, so fixed our souls in a firm growth of union, that no time can eat into the pledge. We would have enjoyed the sweet things our vows expected, had not cruelty — the result of Thrasus' untimely death — prevented all those celebrations we prepared for."

"That is definitely true," Crotolon said.

"From this time sprouted up that poisonous stalk of poisonous aconite, whose ripened fruit has ravished and taken away all health, all comfort of a happy life," Orgilus said, "because Ithocles, Penthea's brother, proud of youth, and prouder in his power, nourished secretly the memory of former unhappiness, and desired to glory in revenge. Partly by cunning, and partly by threats, he suddenly persuaded and forced his virtuous sister to agree to a marriage with Bassanes, a nobleman, who is in honor and riches, I confess, beyond my fortunes. He ranks higher and is much richer than I."

"None of this is a sound reason to importune my leave for your departure to Athens," Crotolon said.

"Now the sound reason follows," Orgilus replied. "Beauteous Penthea, wedded to this torture by an insulting, arrogant brother, being secretly compelled to yield her virgin freedom up to a man who never can usurp her heart, a heart that was previously contracted to be mine, is now so yoked to a man of the most barbarous thralldom, misery, affliction, that he does not enjoy humanity whose sorrow melts into pity in hearing just her name. He feels sorrow for himself, but he does not like anyone who feels pity for her."

"Explain, please," Crotolon requested.

Orgilus replied, "Bassanes, the man who calls Penthea his wife, considers truly what a heaven of perfections he is lord and husband of when he is thinking that beautiful Penthea is his.

"This thought begets a kind of monster-love that is the nurse to a fear so strong and servile that his jealousy brands all admirers of his wife. All eyes that gaze upon that shrine of beauty — Penthea — he has decided are doing homage to the miracle that is she.

"Someone, he is positive, may now or later, if opportunity only presents itself, prevail over her. Out of a self-unworthiness of her, his fears carry him away entirely. It is not that he finds a reason for his jealousy in her behavior, for she is obedient to him, but he finds the reason for his jealousy in his own distrust."

"You spin out your discourse," Crotolon said. "You are taking a long time to say what you have to say. You have not yet given a sound reason for your wanting to go to Athens."

"My griefs are violent," Orgilus said, "for knowing how the maiden Penthea was previously courted by me, Bassanes' jealousies grow wild with fear that I should steal again into her favors, and undermine her virtues — which the gods know that I neither dare nor dream of.

"Hence, from hence I want to undertake a voluntary exile.

"My first reason is that by my absence I will take away the worries of jealous Bassanes.

"Second, and chiefly, sir, I want to free Penthea from a hell on earth. If I am gone, Bassanes will be less jealous and will treat her better.

"Lastly, I want to lose the memory of something her presence makes live in me afresh. When I see her, I think of what might have been but will never be."

"Enough, my Orgilus, enough," Crotolon said. "Go to Athens. I give you my full consent.

"It's a pity about that good lady — Penthea!

"Shall we hear from you often?"

"Yes," Orgilus said. "Often."

"Look," Crotolon said. "Your sister is coming to give you a farewell."

Euphrania walked over to Orgilus and said, "Brother!"

"Euphrania," Orgilus said, "thus upon your cheeks I print a brother's kiss; I am more concerned about your honor, your health, and your well-doing, than my life. Before we part, in the presence of our father, I must make a request to you."

"My brother, you may call it a command instead of a request," Euphrania replied.

Orgilus said, "What I want is that you will promise to never give to any man, however worthy, your faith and loyalty, until, with our father's permission, I give you my free consent."

"That's an easy request to grant!" Crotolon said. "I'll promise for her, Orgilus."

"I beg your pardon," Orgilus said, "but it is Euphrania's oath that will give me satisfaction."

"By Vesta's sacred fires I swear," Euphrania swore.

Vesta was the goddess of the hearth; virgins — the Vestal virgins — served her.

"And I," Crotolon swore, "by the sunbeams of the great sun-god Apollo, join in the vow. Orgilus, I swear not to bestow her on any living man without your permission."

"Dear Euphrania," Orgilus said, "don't mistake what I am asking. It is far, far from my thoughts, far from any wish of mine, to hinder the promotion of you to an honorable bed or a fitting fortune. You are young and beautiful, and it would be an injustice — more, it would be a tyranny — not to promote your merit.

"Trust me, sister, it shall be my first care to see you matched and married as may become your choice and our happiness.

"Do I have your oath?"

"You have," Euphrania said. "But do you mean, brother, to leave us, as you have said?"

"Yes, yes, Euphrania," Crotolon said. "He has just grounds for his decision to go to Athens. I will prove to be a father and a brother to you."

"Heaven looks into the secrets of all hearts," Euphrania said. "Gods, you have mercy with you, else —"

"Don't be afraid," Crotolon interrupted. "Your brother will return safely to us."

"Souls sunk in sorrows never are without them," Orgilus said. "They may go to a new environment with different air, but they carry their griefs with them."

— 1.2 —

In a room in his palace, Amyclas the Spartan King, Armostes, and Prophilus were meeting. Courtiers and attendants were present. Armostes was a councilor of state, and he was the uncle of Ithocles. Prophilus was a friend to Ithocles, the twin brother of Penthea, with whom Orgilus was in love.

"The Spartan gods are gracious," King Amyclas said. "Our humility shall bend before their altars and perfume their temples with abundant sacrifice.

"See, lords, Amyclas, your old king, is entering into his youth again! I shall shake off this silver badge of age, and exchange this snow for hairs as gay as are Apollo's long, golden locks."

Using the royal plural, King Amyclas added, "Our heart leaps in new vigor."

"May old time run backward to double your long life, great sir!" Armostes said.

"It will, it must, Armostes," King Amyclas said.

King Amyclas then explained the reason for his happiness and youthful vigor: "Your bold nephew, death-defying Ithocles, brings to our gates triumphs and peace upon his conquering sword. Laconia is a monarchy at length."

He meant that now Laconia, aka Lacedaemon, was a unified monarchy. The Spartans had defeated their neighboring enemies, the Messenians, and so Messenia, whose capital was Messene, was now a Spartan province. The Spartans had fought more than one war with Messenia.

King Amyclas continued, "Ithocles has in this latter war trod under foot Messene's pride; Messene bows her neck to Lacedaemon's royalty.

"Oh, it was a glorious victory, and it deserves more than a chronicle of history — it deserves a temple, lords, a temple to the name of Ithocles."

He then asked Ithocles' friend, "Where did you leave Ithocles, Prophilus?"

"At Pephon, most gracious sovereign," Prophilus said.

Pephon was a town on the border of Sparta and Messenia.

Prophilus continued, "Twenty of the noblest of the Messenians there wait at your pleasure for such conditions as you shall propose in settling peace, and liberty of life."

King Amyclas asked, "When will your friend, the general, come?"

Prophilus replied, "He promised to follow with all convenient speed."

7

Calantha, Euphrania, Chrystalla, and Philema, all females, arrived. Crotolon, the father of Orgilus, accompanied them. Chrystalla and Philema were carrying a wreath.

Calantha was the daughter of King Amyclas. Chrystalla and Philema were Calantha's female attendants. Euphrania was Orgilus' sister and Crotolon's daughter.

"Our daughter!" King Amyclas said. "Dear Calantha, has the happy news about the conquest of Messene already enriched your knowledge?"

"Yes," Calantha replied. "Prophilus himself has faithfully related the circumstances and manner of the fight."

She then asked Prophilus, "But, please, sir, tell me how does the youthful general Ithocles conduct his actions in these fortunes? How is he behaving?"

Many young men could become bigheaded with such early success.

"Excellent princess," Prophilus replied, "your own beautiful eyes may soon report a truth to your judgment, a truth about with what moderation, calmness of nature, measure, bounds, and limits of thankfulness and joy, he digests such amplitude of his success as would in others, who are molded with a spirit less clear, advance them to compare themselves with heaven. But Ithocles —"

"— your friend," Calantha said.

Prophilus' praise of Ithocles was very high, and Calantha knew that Prophilus' friendship with Ithocles might account for some of that praise.

Prophilus replied, "He is my friend, indeed, madam, and in that friendship the high point of my fate consists. Ithocles, in this firmament of honor, stands like a fixed star, not moved with any thunder of popular applause or sudden lightning of self-opinion; he has served his country, and thinks it was only his duty to do so."

This society believed that the planets and stars were embedded in spheres around the sun. The fixed stars did not change position in relation to each other; in contrast, the planets wandered in the sky.

"You describe a miracle of man," Crotolon said.

"Such, Crotolon," King Amyclas said, "I say on a king's word, you will find him. If Ithocles is not as he has been described, I have perjured myself."

Trumpets sounded.

"Listen, this is the announcement of Ithocles' arrival!" King Amyclas said. "All wait on him."

Ithocles and the courtiers Hemophil and Groneas arrived. The rest of the lords escorted Ithocles over to King Amyclas.

"Return into these arms, your home, your sanctuary," King Amyclas said, "you delight of Sparta, treasure of my bosom — my own, own Ithocles!"

"I am your humblest subject," Ithocles replied.

His uncle, Armostes, said, "Proud of the blood I claim an interest in, as brother to your mother, I embrace you, very noble nephew."

Ithocles said, "Sir, your love's too partial and biased."

Crotolon said, "Our country speaks through me, who on account of your valor, wisdom, and service shares in this great action giving to you, in part payment of your due merits, a general welcome."

"You exceed in giving me bounty," Ithocles said.

Calantha said, "Chrystalla, Philema, give me the wreath."

She took the wreath from them and said, "Ithocles, upon the wings of Fame the singular and chosen fortune of a high attempt is borne so past the view of common sight, that I myself with my own hands have wrought, to crown your temples, this provincial wreath."

Ithocles had added Messenia as a province to Sparta; the provincial wreath recognized this fact.

She continued, "Accept, wear, and enjoy it as our gift. This is something you deserve as a gift of honor; it is not something you casually acquired."

She placed the wreath on his head. Such wreaths were earned by accomplishing great deeds.

"You are a royal maiden," Ithocles said.

"She is in everything our daughter," King Amyclas said.

"Let me blush," Ithocles said, "acknowledging how poorly I have served, what nothings I have done, compared with the honors heaped on the issue of a willing mind. In that lay my ability, in that only."

He meant that his mind was eagerly willing to serve King Amyclas, and this willingness had resulted in victory in battle.

Ithocles continued, "For who is so sluggish from his birth, so little worthy of a name or country, who owes not out of gratitude for life a debt of service of whatsoever kind the safety or counsel of the commonwealth requires for payment? All men must recognize that they owe service to their country."

"He speaks the truth," Calantha said.

Ithocles said, "Frenzied applause runs to the man whom heaven is pleased to make victorious, and like the drunken priests in Bacchus' sacrifices, without reason, frenzied applause calls the leader-on a demi-god."

The leader-on is the leading priest of Bacchus, or analogously the general of an army.

Ithocles continued, "But it is true, indeed, that each common soldier's blood drops down like legal coin in that hard purchase just like the blood of nobles would whose much more delicate condition has sucked the milk of ease.

"Judgment commands, but resolution executes."

Ithocles was giving credit where credit was due. Yes, he was the general and he had given orders, but the common soldiers who had carried out those orders deserved much credit.

Analogously, however, Ithocles deserved credit, too. King Amyclas had ordered him to be the general of the Spartan army in the war of Messenia and Ithocles had carried out that order.

Many well-ordered organizations have a commanding officer and an executive officer. The commanding officer makes the important decisions, and the executive officer makes sure that they are carried out.

Ithocles was wary of insulting King Amyclas, the commanding officer.

He said, "I use not, in this royal presence of the king, these fit slights — these appropriately belittling terms — as being in contempt of such as can command others.

"My speech has a different purpose: I do not wish to attribute all praise to one man's good fortune — a good fortune that is strengthened by the work of many hands.

"For instance, here is Prophilus, a gentleman — I cannot flatter when I state what is the truth — of much desert. In addition, although they are of another rank — they are courtiers — both Hemophil and Groneas were not missing to wish their country's peace. In a word, all who were present there did strive their best in the battle, and it was our duty."

Hemophil and Groneas were of a lower social class than Ithocles and Prophilus.

King Amyclas said, "Courtiers turned soldiers!"

A courtier is an attendant at court; attendants are servants, but courtiers and other noble attendants who wait on royalty are much higher ranking than ordinary servants.

Using the royal plural, King Amyclas said to Hemophil and Groneas, "We vouchsafe our hand."

He held out his hand, and Hemophil and Groneas kissed it.

King Amyclas said to them, "Observe your great example. Take notice of the great example that Ithocles provides you."

Hemophil said, "With all diligence."

Groneas said, "Obsequiously and hourly."

"Some repose and relaxation after these toils is needed," King Amyclas said. "We must think about conditions for the conquered; they await them.

"Let's go!

"Come with me, my Ithocles."

Euphrania said to Prophilus, who had attempted to take her arm, "Sir, with your pardon, I do not need a supporter."

Prophilus said, "Fate instructs me."

Did he mean that he was fated to pursue Euphrania?

As people exited, the male courier Hemophil stopped the female attendant Chrystalla, and the male courier Groneas stopped the female attendant Philema. All of these people were high-ranking attendants at the court.

Chrystalla asked Hemophil, "What do you want with me?"

Philema said to Groneas, "Indeed, I dare not stay."

Hemophil said to Chrystalla, "Sweet lady, soldiers are blunt — I want your lips."

Chrystalla replied, "Bah, this is rudeness. When you went away from here, you were not such creatures."

Groneas said, "The spirit of valor is of a mounting nature."

"Mounting" means "aspiring," but the two couriers were aspiring to sexually mount the two female attendants. Perhaps the lips Hemophil wanted from Chrystalla included her labia.

Philema said, "It appears so."

She added, "Please, tell me truthfully how many men apiece have you two been the death of?"

Groneas replied, "By my faith, not many. We were composed of mercy."

Hemophil said, "As for our daring, you heard General Ithocles' praise of us in front of the king."

Chrystalla indirectly quoted Ithocles, "You wished your country's peace."

She added, "That showed your charity, but where are your spoils, such as the soldier fights for?"

Philema said, "They are coming."

Chrystalla said, "By the next carrier, aren't they?"

Groneas said, "Sweet Philema, when I was in the part thickest with my enemies, slashing off one man's head, another's nose, another's arms and legs —"

Philema interrupted, "— and all together."

Groneas continued, "— then I would with a sigh remember you, and cry, 'Dear Philema, it is for your sake that I do these deeds of wonder!'

"Don't you love me with all your heart now?"

Philema said, "I love you as much now as I did before. I have not put my love out in usury; the principal will hardly yield any interest."

Groneas said, "By Mars, I'll marry you!"

Philema replied, "By Vulcan, you're forsworn."

Mars, god of war, had cuckolded Vulcan by sleeping with Vulcan's wife, Venus.

Philema continued, "Unless my mind strangely changes itself, you've perjured yourself by saying that you'll marry me."

Groneas said, "One word."

"You lie beyond all modesty," Chrystalla said, "Leave me alone."

Hemophil said to her, "I'll make you the mistress of a city; the city is my own by conquest."

"Make it yours by petition," Chrystalla said. "Sue for it *in forma pauperis*."

"*In forma pauperis*" means "as a pauper." Paupers could sue without paying legal fees.

She continued, "City! You mean kennel."

She then said to both Hemophil and Groneas, "Gallants, take off your courtiers' feathers. Instead, put on aprons, gallants. Learn to wind thread and weave, or learn to trim a lady's dog, and be good, quiet souls of peace, hobgoblins!"

Hobgoblins are tricky, annoying imps.

Hemophil said, "Chrystalla!"

Chrystalla said, "Practice to drill hogs in military formations, in hope to share in the acorns. Soldiers! You are corn-cutters who cut off corns from feet, but you are not as valiant as corn-cutters. They often draw blood, which you dare never do.

"When you have practiced more intelligence or more civility, we'll rank you in the list of men. Until then, brave things-at-arms, don't dare to speak to us."

She added sarcastically, "Most potent Groneas!"

Philema said sarcastically, "And Hemophil the hardy! We are at your services."

Chrystalla and Philema exited.

Groneas said, "They scorn us just as they did before we went to war."

"Hang them!" Hemophil said. "Let's scorn them, and be revenged."

"Shall we?" Groneas asked.

"We will," Hemophil said, "and when we slight them thus, instead of us following them, they'll follow us. It is a woman's nature to do that."

Groneas said, "It is a scurvy nature."

The gardens of the palace included a grove. The philosopher Tecnicus and Orgilus, who was disguised like one of Tecnicus' pupils, talked together within that grove. Orgilus was holding a book.

Tecnicus said, "Tempt not the stars; young man, you can not play with the severity of fate. This change of clothing and outward disguise does not hide the secrets of the soul within you from the stars' quick-piercing eyes, which dive at all times down to your thoughts. In your aspect — face and horoscope — I note an augury of danger."

As Tecnicus had talked to the disguised Orgilus, he had looked sometimes at Orgilus and sometimes at the stars to find out what they foretold about the disguised Orgilus' future.

The disguised Orgilus replied, "Give me permission, grave and distinguished Tecnicus, without foredooming destiny — without telling me that I have an evil future — under your roof to ease my silent griefs, by applying to my hidden wounds the balm of your oracular lectures.

"If my fortune were to run such a crooked by-way as to wrest my steps to ruin, yet your learned precepts shall call me back and set my footings straight.

"I will not court the world."

The disguised Orgilus was saying that Tecnicus' wisdom could help him overcome whatever evil fortune lay in store for him. He was also saying that he would be a diligent student and shun worldly pleasures.

"Ah, Orgilus," Tecnicus replied, "neglects in young men of delights and life run often to extremities; young men who have contempt for their own harms are not concerned about harms to others."

Tecnicus was wise. Young men who shun worldly pleasures can end up being extremists. Being contemptuous of the things they are deprived of, they will not have empathy for others who are deprived of things they want or need.

The disguised Orgilus replied, "But I, most learned scholar, am not so much at odds with nature that I will behave unnaturally and will grudge the prosperity of any true deserver. In addition, the misfortunes afflicting my present hopes do not so check my hopes with discouragement and despair that

I am yielding or will yield to thoughts of more affliction than what is incident to human frailty and weakness.

"Therefore, do not think that this retired course of living I wish to undertake for some little time is due to any other cause than what I justly tell you: I have an unsettled mind, as the effect on me must clearly witness. Simply by seeing and talking to me, you must realize that my mind is now unsettled."

"May the spirit of truth inspire you," Tecnicus said. "On these conditions we have talked about, I will conceal and not reveal your disguise, and I will willingly admit you as my student.

"I'll go now to my study."

"I will go to my contemplations in these delightful walks," the disguised Orgilus said.

Tecnicus exited.

Alone, the disguised Orgilus said to himself, "Thus metamorphosed and disguised, I may without suspicion inquire about Penthea's treatment and Euphrania's faith.

"Love, you are full of mystery! The deities themselves are not safe and free from anxiety in searching out the secrets of those flames, which, hidden, waste a breast made tributary to the laws of beauty. Medicine has never yet found a remedy to cure a lover's wound."

Hearing a noise, he asked himself, "Who are those people who cross yonder private walk and go into the shadowing grove in amorous togetherness?"

Prophilus was walking with Euphrania. He was supporting her arm, and he was whispering to her.

The disguised Orgilus said to himself, "My sister! Oh, my sister! It is Euphrania with Prophilus. He is supporting her arm, too! I wish that it were an apparition! Prophilus is Ithocles' friend. This strangely puzzles me."

They walked out of sight briefly and then returned.

"Again!" the disguised Orgilus said to himself. "Help me, my book; this scholar's clothing must serve as my excuse for being in this garden. My mind is busy, and my eyes and ears are open."

He began to read the book he was holding.

Prophilus said to Euphrania, "Do not waste the span of this stolen time, lent to us by the gods for precious use, in over-particular and coy scruples.

Bright Euphrania, if I would repeat old vows, or study new vows for the acquisition of belief to my desires —"

The disguised Orgilus thought, *Desires!*

Prophilus continued, " — my service, my integrity —"

The disguised Orgilus thought, *That's better.*

Prophilus continued, "— I would only repeat a lesson often memorized without any prompter but your eyes: My love is honorable."

The disguised Orgilus thought, *So was my love for my Penthea. My love was chastely honorable.*

Prophilus continued, "Nor is there lacking any more addition to my wish of happiness than having you for my wife. I am already sure that Ithocles is my firm and unalterable friend."

The disguised Orgilus thought, *But Ithocles is a brother crueler than the grave. He was cruel when he made Penthea — his sister — marry a brute.*

Euphrania replied to Prophilus, "What can you look for, in answer to your noble protestations, from an inexperienced maiden, except language suited to a divided mind?"

The disguised Orgilus thought, *Hold out, Euphrania!*

Euphrania said, "Know, Prophilus, that from the first time you mentioned worthy love, I never undervalued your merit, means, or person. It would have been a fault of judgment in me, and a dullness in my affections, not to weigh and thank my better stars that offered me the grace of so much blissfulness. For, to say the truth, the law of my desires kept equal pace with yours, nor have I left that resolution.

"But briefly I must say that whatever choice of a husband lives nearest in my heart must first procure consent from both my father and my brother, before my choice can call me his."

The disguised Orgilus thought, *She is forsworn else. If she does not get my father's consent and my consent, she will perjure herself.*

Prophilus said, "Leave to me that task. I will get the necessary consent."

Euphrania said, "I gave my brother, before he departed to Athens, my oath that I would not marry without his consent."

The disguised Orgilus thought, *Yes, yes, he — I — received her oath, certainly.*

Prophilus said, "I don't doubt that, with the means the court supplies, I will do otherwise than prevail at pleasure. I don't doubt that I will marry you."

The disguised Orgilus thought, *Very likely!*

Prophilus continued, "In the meantime, best, dearest, I may build my hopes on the foundation of your constant love for me despite any opposition that may arise to our being married."

Euphrania replied, "Death shall sooner divorce life and the joys I have in living than my chaste vows from truth."

She meant two things: 1) She would remain in love with Prophilus, and 2) She would not marry him unless she had the consent of her father and her brother.

Understanding only the first thing she meant, Prophilus said, "On your fair hand I seal the same promise."

He kissed her hand.

Understanding only the first thing she meant, the disguised Orgilus thought, *There is no faith in any woman.*

Then he murmured to himself, "Passion, oh, be contained! Strong emotion, be restrained! My heartstrings are being stretched on tenterhooks."

Euphrania said to Prophilus, "Sir, we are overheard. May Cupid protect us! Someone nearby made a stirring, sir."

"Your fears are needless, lady," Prophilus said. "No one has access to these private pleasure walks except some people who are nearby in court, or some favorite student from Tecnicus' oratory — that place for practicing public speaking — granted by special favor recently from King Amyclas to the grave, serious philosopher."

Euphrania said, "I think I hear someone talking to himself — I see him."

Prophilus looked and saw the disguised Orgilus with his book and said, "He is a poor scholar, as I told you, lady."

The disguised Orgilus thought, *I have been discovered.*

He then said, half aloud to himself, pretending to be arguing with an imaginary opponent, "Say it: Is it possible, with a smooth tongue, a leering countenance, flattery, or force of reason — I see what you are doing, sir — to turn or to appease the raging sea? Answer me that. ... Your art! What art is it to catch and hold fast in a net the small motes in the air that are revealed by sunshine? No, no; they'll out, they'll out. You may as easily outrun a cloud driven by a northern blast as fiddle-faddle such nonsense as this! Shut up, or speak sense."

Euphrania said to Prophilus, "Do you call this thing a scholar? It's a pity, but he's a lunatic."

Prophilus said, "Humor him, sweetheart. This is only his recreation."

The disguised Orgilus continued to pretend to argue with an imaginary opponent: "But will you hear a little? You're so irritable; you keep no rule in argument. Philosophy works not upon impossibilities, but upon natural conclusions. — Bah! — This is absurd! The metaphysics are but speculations about and observations of the celestial bodies, or else such accidents (rather than substances) as are not mixed perfectly, in the air engendered, appear to us as unnatural — that's all. Prove it, yet with a reverence to your gravity, I'll shun illiterate and uninformed sauciness, submitting my sole opinion to the touchstone — test — of writers."

Prophilus said to Euphrania, "Now let us go over and talk to him."

They walked over to him.

The disguised Orgilus continued to pretend to argue with an imaginary opponent, "Ha, ha, ha! These apish boys, when they just taste the rudiments and principles of theory, imagine that they can oppose their teachers. False confidence leads many into errors."

"Excuse me, sir," Prophilus said to the disguised Orgilus.

"Are you a scholar, friend?" Euphrania asked the disguised Orgilus.

"With the pardon of your deities, gay creature," the disguised Orgilus said, "I am a mushroom — a lowly person — on whom the dew of heaven drops now and then. The sun shines on me, too — I thank his beams! Sometimes I feel their warmth, and I eat and sleep."

"Does Tecnicus lecture you?" Prophilus asked.

"Yes, indeed," the disguised Orgilus replied. "He is definitely my master; yonder door opens upon his study."

"Happy creatures!" Prophilus said, referring to scholars, and talking to Euphrania. "Such people toil not, sweetheart, in the heats of matters of state, nor sink in thaws of greatness. Their affections keep order with the limits of their moderation and their modest position in life. Their love is the love of virtue."

He then asked the disguised Orgilus, "What's your name?"

"Aplotes, sumptuous master," the disguised Orgilus said. "I am a poor wretch."

"Aplotes" means Simplicity.

"Do you want anything?" Euphrania asked.

"Books, Venus, books," the disguised Orgilus said.

Venus is the beautiful goddess of sexual passion and of love. Orgilus wanted Venus — to be married to Penthea — but he was also saying that Euphrania, his sister, is metaphorically a beautiful goddess.

Prophilus said to Euphrania, "Lady, a new idea comes into my thought, and it is an idea that will be very useful for making both of us happy."

Euphrania began, "My lord —"

Prophilus interrupted, "While I endeavor to deserve your father's blessing to our loves, this scholar may at some certain hours daily wait here in this grove for whatever note I can write about my success, and give the note to your hands. You can also use him to give notes to me. That way, we can never be barred from communicating with each other, we will never lack sure and certain information about each other, and our hearts may talk to each other when our tongues cannot."

"This opportunity is very favorable," Euphrania said. "Make use of it."

Prophilus said, "Aplotes, will you wait for either of us twice a day, at nine in the morning and at four in the afternoon, here in this bower, to convey such letters as each of us shall send to the other? Do it willingly, safely, and secretly, and I will furnish you what you need for study, or whatever else you desire."

"Jove, make me thankful, thankful, I beseech you, propitious Jove!" the disguised Orgilus said.

Jove is Jupiter, the king of gods.

The disguised Orgilus continued, "I will prove to be sure and trusty. You will not fail to provide me with books?"

"Nor with anything else your heart can desire," Prophilus replied. "This lady's name is Euphrania, and my name is Prophilus."

"I have a good memory," the disguised Orgilus said. "It must prove to be my best friend. I will not miss one minute of the hours appointed."

Prophilus said, "Write down a list of the books you want me to bring you, or take some money."

"No, no money," the disguised Orgilus said. "Money to scholars is an invisible spirit. We dare not touch it. Either give me books, or nothing."

"I will bring you books of whatever sort you want," Prophilus said. "Do not forget our names."

"I promise you that I will not forget your names," the disguised Orgilus said.

Prophilus said, "Smile, Hymen, on the growth of our desires. We'll feed your torches with eternal fires!"

Hymen is the god of marriage. His symbol is a bridal torch.

Prophilus and Euphrania exited.

"Put out your torches, Hymen, or their light shall meet a darkness of eternal night!" the disguised Orgilus said to himself. "Inspire me, Mercury, with swift deceits."

Mercury is the god of thieves.

At this time, Orgilus was opposed to marriage between his sister and Prophilus.

He continued talking to himself, "Ingenious Fate has leapt into my arms and has given me an opportunity beyond what I could have planned.

"Mortals creep on the dung of earth, and cannot understand the riddles that are purposed by the gods.

"Great acts best write themselves in their own stories; people die too basely who outlive their glories."

Stoics believed that when existence becomes humiliating, suicide is an ethical act.

CHAPTER 2

— 2.1 —

Bassanes and Phulas, one of his servants, talked together in a room in Bassanes' house.

"I'll have that window next to the street blocked up," Bassanes said. "It gives too full a prospect to temptation, and it courts a gazer's glances."

His wife, Penthea, sometimes sat by that window. Jealous Bassanes was afraid that she could be tempted to commit adultery with someone she saw outside the window; he also worried that someone outside could see Penthea through the window and lust after her.

Bassanes continued, "There's a lust committed by the eye, which sweats and travails, plots, wakes, and contrives until the deformed bear-whelp — adultery — be licked into the act, the very act."

According to Pliny, the mother bear licked her newborn cubs into shape.

Matthew 5:28 states, *"But I say unto you, That whosoever looketh on a woman to lust after her hath committed adultery with her already in his heart"* (King James Version).

Bassanes continued, "That light — that window — shall be dammed up, do you hear, sir?"

"I do hear, my lord," Phulas replied. "A mason shall be provided to do the work immediately."

Bassanes said, "Some rogue, some rogue of your confederacy — an agent for slaves and strumpets! — to convey secret letters from this spruce youth and to other youngsters, that gaudy flatterer, your patron who gives you money —"

Bassanes was so angry at the thought of Phulas being bribed to carry letters to his wife that he had to stop speaking. Recovering, he said, "I'll tear your throat out, you son of a cat, you ill-looking hound's-head, and I'll rip up your ulcerous mouth, if I only scent a paper, a scroll, just half as big as what can cover a wart upon your nose, a spot, a pimple — if I only scent a piece of a letter directed to my wife; it may prove to be a secret preparation for lewdness."

Phulas said, "Care shall be taken: I will turn every thread about me into an eye."

Argos was an ancient god with a hundred eyes all over his body.

Phulas thought, sarcastically, *Here's a sweet life!*

Bassanes said, "The city housewives, cunning in the traffic of chamber merchandise, set all at wholesale prices."

"Chamber merchandise" is sex for sale. According to Bassanes, the city housewives sold sex at wholesale prices — that is, cheap.

Bassanes continued, "Yet the city housewives wipe their mouths and simper, embrace, kiss, and cry, 'Sweetheart,' and stroke the head that they have made branch with the horns of a cuckold, and all is well again!"

This society joked that cuckolds — men with unfaithful wives — had invisible horns growing from their forehead.

Bassanes continued, "The city housewives' husbands are dull clods of dirt who dare not feel the impediments stuck on their foreheads."

"It is a villainous world," Phulas said. "One cannot hold his own in it."

"Dames at court, who flaunt themselves in riotous behavior, run in another direction," Bassanes said. "Their pleasure heaves the patient, suffering ass — their husband — up on the stilts of office, titles, incomes. Promotion to success justifies the shame of cuckoldry, and the husbands beg to be cuckolded. Poor honor, you are stabbed by and bleed to death because of such unlawful use of lawfully wedded wives!

"The country mistress is yet more wary, and in blushes she hides whatever trespass draws her truth to guilt.

"But all women are false and unfaithful: Of this truth I am firmly convinced. No woman can do anything other than fall and be unfaithful, and either she does fall and is unfaithful, or she wants to fall and be unfaithful."

Bassanes had a clear opinion about *all* women.

He then said, "Now for the newest news about the city. What are the voices blabbing, sirrah?"

"Oh, my lord," Phulas said, "the rarest, quaintest, strangest, tickling news that ever —"

"Come on!" Bassanes said. "Hurry up and tell me, rascal! What is it?"

"Indeed, they say the king has molted all his gray beard, in place of which he has grown another of a pure pink-flesh color, speckled with green and russet."

"Ignorant blockhead!" Bassanes said.

"Yes, truly," Phulas said, "and it is talked about the streets that, since Lord Ithocles came home, the lions have never stopped roaring, at which noise the dancing bears have danced their very hearts out."

"Dance your heart out, too," Bassanes said.

"In addition, Lord Orgilus has fled to Athens upon a fiery dragon," Phulas said, "and it is thought that he can never return."

"Grant that he never return, Apollo!" Bassanes prayed.

"Moreover, if it please your lordship," Phulas said, "it is reported as certain that whoever is found jealous without apparent proof that his wife is wanton shall be divorced — but this is but she-news. I heard it from a midwife. I have more news still."

"Fool, speak no more!" Bassanes said. "Idiots and stupid fools irritate my calamities. Why, to be fair should yield presumption of a faulty soul — all beautiful women should be thought to have a faulty soul."

He stopped and then said, "Look after the doors."

He wanted them to be securely locked so that a man could not creep in and cuckold him.

Phulas thought, *May the horn of plenty crest him!*

The horn of plenty is a cornucopia, but Phulas was conflating it with a cuckold's horns. His meaning was, *May Bassanes be cuckolded many times!*

Phulas exited to carry out his orders.

Bassanes said to himself, "Swarms of confusion huddle and crowd in my thoughts in rare distemper. Beauty! Oh, it is either an unmatched blessing or a horrid curse."

Penthea and Grausis entered the room. Grausis, who was an old lady, was Penthea's servant.

Seeing Penthea, Bassanes said to himself, "She comes! She comes! So shoots the morning forth, spangled with pearls of transparent dew. The way to poverty is to be rich, as I in her am wealthy; but because of her, I am bankrupt when it comes to happiness."

He said out loud, "Beloved Penthea! How fares my heart's best joy?"

Grausis said, "Truly, she is not well. She is so excessively sad."

"Stop chattering, magpie," Bassanes said to Grausis.

Then he said to his wife, Penthea, "Your brother has returned, sweet, safe, and honored with a triumphant victory. You shall visit him.

"We will go to court, where, if it be your pleasure, you shall appear in such a ravishing luster of jewels above value that the dames who show off their fine jewels there, because of rage at being so outshined by you, shall hide themselves in their closets and unseen fret in their tears, while every wondering eye shall crave no other brightness but your presence.

"Choose your own recreations and entertainments. Be a queen of whatever delights you fancy best — choose what company, what place, what times. Do anything, do all things that youth can command, so that you will chase these clouds from the pure firmament of your beautiful looks."

His words did not match his jealousy. He was saying good-sounding things, but if his wife were to do what he was advising her to do, he would be insanely jealous — and both he and she knew it. He did not mean what he said.

"Now that is well said, my lord," Grausis said.

She then said to Penthea, "What, lady! Laugh, and be merry; time is precious."

Bassanes thought, *May Furies whip you!*

The Furies are avenging goddesses of ancient Greece.

Penthea said, "Alas, my lord and husband, this language to your handmaid sounds like music would to the deaf."

She knew that her husband, Bassanes, was jealous, and she knew that he would be jealous if she were to do as he said and dress splendidly and show herself to others, including other men. She also regarded herself as a handmaid to her husband; her role was to serve her husband.

She continued, "I need no splendid displays of jewels and no cost of art to draw the whiteness of my name and reputation into offence."

If she were to wear jewels and makeup, her husband would be jealous. That was not something she needed. Indeed, her husband was jealous even when she was not wearing jewels or makeup and even when she was alone.

She continued, "Let such women, if any such women exist who covet a pursuit of admiration by displaying their plenty to the full view of others, appear in gaudy clothing and jewels.

"My clothing shall suit the inward fashion of my mind."

Her mind was somber, and so would be her clothing.

She continued, "I believe that, if your opinion, nobly placed, does not change the livery your words bestow, my fortunes with my hopes are at the highest."

"Livery" was the clothing that a servant wore; she regarded herself as her husband's servant. Unless her husband's opinion of her changed — his opinion was that she was eager to cuckold him — and thereby changed his and her relationship, then her fortunes with her hopes are at the highest.

Why are her fortunes and her hopes "at the highest"? Because as low as they are now, unless her husband changes, they will never get higher.

Bassanes, still jealous, said, "This house, I think, stands somewhat too secluded. It is too melancholy; we'll move closer to the court. Or what does my Penthea think about the delightful island we command? Rule me as you can wish. Tell me what you want."

Penthea said, "I am no mistress."

A mistress is a female head of a household. Most wives are mistresses in this sense, but Penthea was not. She did not have a say in the house in which she lived. She would not have ordered the window she sat at to be blocked up.

She continued, "Whatever you want, I must obey you; all ways are alike pleasant to me."

Grausis said, "Island! Prison! A prison is as gay as an island. We'll have no islands. By the Virgin Mary, out upon them! Damn them! Whom shall we see on an island? Seagulls, and porpoises, and water rats, and crabs, and more seagulls, and dogfish. This is 'goodly' gear for a young lady's friendly intercourse — or an old one's! On no terms will we have islands; I'll be stewed first."

"Stewed" meant "sent to the brothels, aka stews."

Bassanes whispered, "Grausis, you are a juggling bawd."

He would be happy to have his wife on an island; the surrounding water would make it harder for men to cuckold him.

He said out loud to his wife, "This sadness, sweetest wife, does not become youthful blood."

He whispered to Grausis, "I'll have you impounded."

He said out loud to his wife, "For my sake put on a more cheerful mirth. If you don't, you'll mar your cheeks, and make me old in griefs."

He whispered to Grausis, "You damnable bitch-fox!"

Grausis whispered back, "I am always hard of hearing when the wind blows from the south."

A wind blowing from the south to the north is metaphorically a low wind. Grausis disliked disagreeable thoughts and did not want to hear them when they were directed verbally at her.

She said out loud to him, "What do you think if your fresh lady would breed young bones, my lord? Wouldn't a strapping boy do you good at heart?"

Her words were ambiguous: 1) Penthea could breed with Bassanes and give birth to a healthy boy, or 2) Penthea could breed with a strapping young man who was not Bassanes.

She continued, "But, as you said —"

Interrupting, Bassanes whispered to Grausis, "I'll spit you on a stake, or chop you into slices of meat!"

"Please, speak louder," Grausis said. "Surely, surely the wind is still blowing from the south."

Penthea said, "You babble madly."

Bassanes replied, "It is very hot; I sweat extremely."

Sweat was thought in this society to be a sign of jealousy.

Phulas returned.

"Now what is it?" Bassanes asked.

"A herd of lords, sir," Phulas replied.

"Huh!" Bassanes said.

"A flock of ladies," Phulas said.

"Where?" Bassanes asked.

"Shoals of horses," Phulas said.

Normally, we speak of herds of cattle, flocks of birds, and shoals of fish.

"Peasant, what are you talking about?" Bassanes said.

"Coaches in drifts and droves," Phulas said.

Normally, we speak of droves of cattle. At this time, people also spoke of drifts of cattle; cattle in a forest would be driven to a particular place on a particular day so that such things as ownership of the cattle could be determined.

"One person enters, the other group of people stands outside, sir," Phulas said. "And now I vanish."

He exited.

Prophilus, Hemophil, Groneas, Chrystalla, and Philema entered the room.

"Noble Bassanes!" Prophilus greeted him.

"You are very welcome, Prophilus," Bassanes said. "Ladies, gentlemen, to all my heart is open; you all honor me —"

He thought, *A swelling affects my head already.*

He may have thought of horns swelling on his forehead.

He continued, "— honor me bountifully."

He thought, *How they flutter, wagtails and jays together!*

Wagtails are promiscuous women, and jays are chatterers.

Prophilus said to Penthea, "Your brother, by virtue of your love to him, asked that I request your immediate presence, fairest lady. He wants to see you."

"Ithocles is well, sir?" Penthea asked.

"May the gods preserve him forever!" Prophilus said, "Yet, dear beauty, I find some alteration in him lately, since his return to Sparta."

He then said to Bassanes, "My good lord, please, do not delay in allowing her to see her brother."

Bassanes replied, "We would not have needed an invitation, if his sister's health had not fallen into question."

He then said, "Make haste, Penthea; don't slacken even a minute."

"Lead the way, good Prophilus," Penthea said. "I'll follow step by step."

"Give me your arm, fair madam," Prophilus said to Penthea.

All exited except Bassanes and Grausis.

Bassanes said, "I require one word with your old bawdship. It would have been better for you to have railed against the sins you worship than to have thwarted my will. I wanted to go and live on the island. I'll treat you cursedly."

"You dote," Grausis said. "You are foolish. You are beside yourself. You think that you are a politician — a schemer — in jealousy? No, you are too gross, too vulgar. Pish, don't try to teach me my job; I know what to do and when to do it. My thwarting your will sinks me deeper into her trust — she trusts me now more than before. By means of her trust in me, I shall know everything; my trade's a sure one — I will know what you want me to know about her."

"Forgive me, Grausis," Bassanes said. "What you said is something that I did not realize. But be careful now."

"Don't worry. I am no new-come-to-it," Grausis said. "I am no newcomer."

"Your life rests upon it, and so does mine," Bassanes said. "My agonies are infinite."

Ithocles stood alone in his apartment in the palace.

He said to himself, "Ambition! It is like the vipers' breed: It gnaws a passage through the womb that gave it motion."

This society believed that vipers gave birth when their offspring bit their way out of the mother viper's womb.

He continued, "Ambition, like a released dove blinded by sewing up the eyelids, mounts upward, higher and higher still, in order to perch on clouds, but tumbles headlong down with heavier ruin."

Blinded doves climb higher and higher into the air until, exhausted, they fall to the ground.

He continued, "So squibs and crackers — fireworks — fly into the air, then, breaking with only a noise, they vanish in stench and smoke."

Ithocles was critical of ambition unrestrained by morality, but that need not mean that he felt such ambition. It may mean only that he was aware of the danger and by thinking about it he was taking steps never to have that kind of ambition.

He continued, "Morality, applied to timely practice and present business, keeps the soul healthy. In other words, morality, applied to daily life, keeps the soul in tune. With a soul's healthy and sweet music, all of our actions dance.

"But this is what we learn from books and scholastic philosophy; it will not heal the sickness of a mind that is broken with griefs. Strong fevers are not eased with advice, but with the best recipes for effective medicine and courses of action — speedy courses of action, and certain-to-work courses of action — that's the cure."

Engaged in a discussion, Armostes and Crotolon entered the room. Armostes was a councilor of state, and he was the uncle of Ithocles. Crotolon was the father of Orgilus and Euphrania. The discussion was about whether a marriage between Prophilus and Euphrania should take place.

Armostes said, "You stick, Lord Crotolon, upon a point too picky, too scrupulous, and too unnecessary. Prophilus is in every way full of merit. I am confident that your wisdom is too ripe to need instruction from your son's tutelage."

Crotolon had promised his son, Ithocles, that Euphrania would not marry without Ithocles' consent.

Crotolon replied, "Yet my judgment is not so ripe, my Lord Armostes, that it dares to dote upon the painted meat — the bait — of smooth persuasion, which tempts me to a breach of faith."

Ithocles said to Crotolon, "This question is not yet resolved, my lord? Why, if your son's consent is so efficacious, we will write to Athens for his return to Sparta. The king's hand will join with our desires; he has been persuaded to recall Orgilus."

"Yes," Armostes said, "and the king himself importuned Crotolon to write a dispatch to Orgilus."

"Kings may command," Crotolon said. "Their wills are laws that are not to be questioned."

Crotolon was willing to write the letter. His problem with the marriage was that his son's consent was needed before the marriage took place.

Ithocles said, "By this marriage you will knit a union so devout, so hearty, between your loves to me and mine to yours, as if my own blood had an interest in it, for Prophilus is mine, and I am his."

A marriage between Prophilus and Euphrania would more closely knit Ithocles and Prophilus and the family of Crotolon to each other.

"My lord, my lord!" Crotolon said.

"What, good sir?" Ithocles said. "Speak your thought."

"Had this sincerity of yours been real earlier, my Orgilus had not been now without a wife," Crotolon said, "nor would your lost sister be buried in a bride-bed."

Of course, he was referring to the marriage that had been arranged between Orgilus and Penthea — an arranged marriage that Ithocles had broken off when he made Penthea marry the jealous Bassanes.

"Your uncle here, Armostes, knows that this is the truth," Crotolon said, "for if your father, Thrasus, had lived — but may peace dwell in his grave! I have finished speaking about this."

"You are bold and bitter," Armostes said to Crotolon.

He did not think that the breaking up of the engagement should have been mentioned.

Ithocles thought, *He presses home the injury; it smarts.*

Whom "it smarts" was ambiguous, but it hurt Crotolon and Orgilus and Penthea — and it hurt Ithocles, who felt guilty.

Ithocles said out loud, "No reprehensions, uncle Armostes; I deserve Crotolon's criticism."

He then said to Crotolon, "Yet, gentle sir, consider what the heat of an unsteady youth, a giddy brain, green indiscretion, flattery of greatness, rawness of judgment, the willfulness of folly, thoughts as vagrant as the wind and as uncertain, might lead a boy in years to."

He was blaming his youth, inexperience, flattery by others, and foolishness for the mistake he now acknowledged that he had made. He had been too young to understand strong love.

He continued, "It was a fault, a deadly fault, for then I could not dive into the secrets of commanding love. Since that time, experience, by the extremes — in others — has forced me to have a better understanding."

Ithocles had added "in others" so that his hearers would not know that he himself was in love — with Calantha, the king's daughter.

He added, "And, trust me, Crotolon, I will redeem those wrongs with any service your satisfaction can require for satisfactory redemption."

Armostes said to Crotolon, "Ithocles' acknowledgment is satisfactory. What more could you want?"

"I'm conquered," Crotolon said. "If Euphrania herself allows the engagement, let it be so. I don't doubt that my son will like this marriage."

Ithocles said, "Use my fortunes, life, power, sword, and heart — all are your own."

Armostes said to Ithocles, "Here is the princess, with your sister."

Princess Calantha, Penthea, and Euphrania entered the room, along with Chrystalla, Philema, Grausis, Bassanes, and Prophilus.

Calantha said, "I present to you a stranger here in court, my lord; for if her desire of seeing you did not draw her from her home, we would not have been made happy with her company."

The stranger was his sister, Penthea, who seldom left her home because of her jealous husband.

Ithocles replied, "You, Calantha, are a gracious princess."

Then he said to Penthea, "Sister, wedlock holds too severe a passion in your nature, which can engross all duty to your husband, without attendance on so dear a mistress."

He was pointing out that she was with her husband so much that she was neglecting her duty to Calantha.

Ithocles then said to Bassanes, "It is not my brother-in-law's pleasure, I presume, to immure her in a chamber."

"It is her will," Bassanes lied. "She governs her own hours. Noble Ithocles, we thank the gods for your success and welfare. Our lady Penthea has recently been ill and indisposed, or else we would have been among the first to visit you."

Ithocles asked, "How is my sister — Penthea — doing now?"

Penthea replied, "You best know, brother, from whom my health and comforts are derived."

Ithocles was the person who had persuaded her to marry Bassanes.

Bassanes thought, *I like that answer well: It is serious and modest.* But then he thought, *There may be tricks yet, tricks.*

He whispered, "Keep your eyes open, Grausis!"

Calantha said, "Now, Crotolon, the suit we joined in must not fall and fail by too long a delay."

"Your suit has been granted, princess," Crotolon said, "as far as my part is concerned."

Armostes said, "He has agreed to the marriage on the condition that his son also approves of it."

"Such delay is easy," Calantha said. "Orgilus is sure to be quick to approve of the engagement."

She then said, "May the joys of marriage make you, Prophilus, a proud deserver of Euphrania's love, and may they make her a proud deserver of your merit!"

Prophilus replied, "You are most sweetly gracious!"

Bassanes said, "The joys of marriage are the heaven on earth. They are life's paradise, great princess, the soul's quiet, sinews of concord, strength of harmony, earthly immortality, eternity of pleasures — there are no restoratives that are comparable to a constant, loyal, faithful woman!"

He thought, *But where is she? Where exists a woman who is faithful? It would puzzle all the gods just to create such a new monster.*

He added, "I can speak by way of proof, for I rest in Elysium; marriage is my happiness."

Elysium is where good souls go in the ancient version of the Land of the Dead.

Crotolon asked, "Euphrania, how are you resolved — speak freely — in your affections to this gentleman? Do you love him?"

"Neither more nor less than as his love assures me and makes me confident that he loves me, which his love in fact does," Euphrania replied, "and as long as your liking agrees with my brother's warrants, I cannot but approve this gentleman as being in all points worthy."

Crotolon said, "So, so!"

He then said to Prophilus, "I know your answer."

He knew that Prophilus was eager to marry Euphrania.

Ithocles said, "It would have been a pity to sunder hearts that have so equally consented to love each other."

Orgilus and Penthea also had hearts that had so equally consented to love each other.

Hemophil entered the room with a message.

He said, "Lord Ithocles, King Amyclas commands your presence — and, fairest princess, he commands yours, too."

Calantha said, "We will go to him."

In a hurry, Groneas entered the room and said, "Where are the lords? All must go to the king without delay: The Prince of Argos —"

Out of breath, he paused.

"Well, sir?" Calantha asked.

"— is coming to the court, sweet lady," Groneas finished.

"What!" Calantha said. "The Prince of Argos?"

Groneas replied, "It was my fortune, madam, to enjoy the honor of sharing these happy tidings."

"Penthea!" Ithocles said.

"Brother?" Penthea asked.

Ithocles said, "Let me an hour from now meet you alone within the palace's grove. I have a secret to share with you."

He then said to Prophilus, "Please, friend, escort Penthea there, and take special care that the walks be cleared of anyone who would disturb us."

"I shall," Prophilus said.

What's that? Bassanes thought. *What's going on here?*

Ithocles said to Penthea, "Alone, please be alone."

He then said to Calantha, "I am your servant, princess."

He added, "Onward, my lords!"

Everyone exited except Bassanes, who said to himself, "Alone! Alone! What does he mean by that word 'alone'? Why can't I be there? — Hmm! — He's Penthea's brother. Brothers and sisters are but flesh and blood, and this same damn easy court life is temptation to cause a rebellion in the veins; besides, his fine friend Prophilus must be Penthea's guardian: Why can't Prophilus dispatch a business nimbly before the other come?"

That business would be cuckolding Bassanes.

He continued, "Or — pandering, pandering for one another — be it to sister, mother, wife, cousin, anything — among youths of mettle pandering is in fashion; it is so — stubborn fate!"

He was so insanely jealous that he thought that Ithocles might be offering Penthea sexually to Prophilus. In fact, he soon would not rule out the possibility of incest between Ithocles and Penthea.

Bassanes continued, "But if I should be a cuckold, and can know it, I will be fell, and fell — I will be shrewd, and deadly."

Groneas returned and said, "My lord, you are called for."

"Most heartily I thank you," Bassanes said. "Where's my wife, please?"

"She has retired with the rest of the ladies," Groneas said.

Bassanes replied, "Again, I thank you. There's an old servant with her. Did you see her, too?"

The old servant was Grausis, who acted as a chaperone for Penthea.

Groneas said, "She sits in the anteroom of the king's presence-chamber fast asleep, sir."

"Asleep!" Bassanes said, "Asleep, sir!"

If she was asleep, she could not serve effectively as a chaperone.

"Is your lordship troubled?" Groneas asked. "Will you not go to the king?"

"I am your humblest vassal," Bassanes said.

"I am your servant, my good lord," Groneas replied.

"I follow in your footsteps," Bassanes said.

They exited.

Prophilus and Penthea arrived in the grove in the king's garden.

Prophilus said, "In this walk, lady, your brother will find you. With your permission, allow me to prepare you a little for your meeting with your brother. In his way of living, I have observed recently some kind of slackness to such brisk and cheerful alacrity as his nature and custom once took delight in; sadness grows upon his recreations, a sadness that he hoards in such a determined silence that to question him about the grounds of such sadness will argue little skill in friendship, and less in good manners."

Penthea replied, "Sir, I'm not inquisitive about secrecies without an invitation."

She was willing to respect others' privacy.

Prophilus said, "I beg your pardon, lady. Not a syllable of mine implies so rude a sense. Instead, the drift —"

He was interrupted when Orgilus, still disguised as a scholar, appeared, and so he did not finish what he was saying to Penthea.

Prophilus said to the disguised Orgilus, "Do your best to make this lady merry for an hour."

The disguised Orgilus said, "Your will shall be a law, sir. I will do as you say."

Prophilus exited.

"Please, leave me," Penthea requested of the disguised Orgilus. "I have some private thoughts that I want to consider. You may use the time to consider your own thoughts."

"Speak on, fair nymph," the disguised Orgilus said. "Our souls can dance as well to the music of the spheres as the souls of any who have feasted with the gods."

According to this society, the planets and stars and sun were embedded in spheres around the earth, and the spheres created harmonious music as they moved.

Penthea said, "Your school-terms are too troublesome."

"School-terms" are the philosophic terms used in scholastic philosophy, which engaged in the rigorous analysis of concepts.

The disguised Orgilus continued, "What heaven refines mortality from dross of earth but such as uncompounded beauty hallows with glorified perfection?"

Obviously, this is difficult to understand. We may suspect that Orgilus had disguised himself as a scholar who had studied so much that he was losing his wits.

Perhaps he meant this by his rhetorical question, if in fact his words had meaning: The heaven that can make human beings from the soil of the earth is a heaven that will honor pure, uncompounded, unalloyed beauty with glorified perfection.

Penthea said, "Set your wits in a less wild proportion. Speak more clearly."

The disguised Orgilus said, "Time can never on the white tablet of unguilty faith write counterfeit dishonor."

In other words, those who keep their innocent, unguilty faith and loyalty will in the long run not endure an undeserved dishonor. "In the long run" may refer to Judgment Day, when the innocent will be found innocent, and the guilty will be found guilty.

The disguised Orgilus continued, "Turn those eyes, the arrows of pure love, upon that fire, which once rose to a flame, perfumed with vows as sweetly scented as the incense smoking Vesta's altars; virgin tears (that are like the holiest odors) sprinkled dews to feed them and to increase their fervor."

His words were deliberately obscure, but in other, clearer words, he was saying this: Turn your eyes and look at me, who love and loved you with a love perfumed with vows as sweetly scented as the incense smoking on the altars of the goddess Vesta. My virgin tears, like the holiest odors, sprinkled dews to feed my vows and to increase their fervor.

Penthea said, "Don't be frantic."

The disguised Orgilus said, "All pleasures are only pure imagination, feeding the hungry appetite with smells and the sight of the banquet, while the body pines, not relishing the real taste of food.

"Such is the leanness of a heart divided from the intercourse of troth-contracted loves. No horror should deface that precious figure that is sealed with the lively stamp of souls in full agreement."

Penthea, recognizing that these words applied to her own heart and life, said, "Go away! Some Fury has bewitched your tongue."

The Furies were avenging goddesses of ancient Greece. They pursued people such as those who were guilty of patricide and matricide — people who did not properly respect family relationships.

Penthea continued, "The breath of ignorance, which flies from you, ripens a knowledge in me of afflictions above all endurance. You thing of talk, be gone! Leave now, without making a reply!"

The disguised Orgilus said, "Be just, Penthea, in your commands; when you send forth a sentence of banishment, know first on whom it lights."

As he removed his disguise as a scholar, he said, "Now I take off the shroud in which my cares are folded up from view of common eyes."

Then he asked her, "What is your sentence now? How do you judge me?"

Penthea said, "Rash man! You are laying a blemish on my honor with the hazard of your too-desperate life. You are risking your life in doing this, and your action blemishes my honor as a faithful wife.

"Yet I profess by all the laws of ceremonious wedlock that I have not given even one thought to cheating on my husband since cruelty forced a divorce between my body and my heart. Although I am unhappy in my marriage, yet I am faithful to my husband.

"Why would you fall away from goodness like this? Why are you acting in this way?"

Orgilus said, "Oh, rather examine me, and ask me how I could live to say that I have been much, much wronged.

"It is for your sake that I put on this disguise.

"Dear Penthea, if your soft bosom has not turned to marble, you shall pity our calamities; our previous betrothal confirms to me that you are still mine — I have a claim to you."

Penthea said, "Give me your hand. With both of mine I clasp it thus, and thus I kiss it. Thus I kneel before you."

She knelt before him.

Orgilus said, "You teach me my duty."

He knelt.

Penthea said, "We may stand up."

Previously, they had knelt together, clasped hands, and kissed each other's hand. They had also pledged to be married. This time, no pledge of marriage occurred. This was Penthea's way of telling Orgilus that their previous betrothal was no longer a betrothal and that therefore he had no claim to her.

Penthea said, "Have you anything else to urge of any new demand on me? Do you have any other claim on me? As for your old claim, forget it; it is buried in an everlasting silence, and it shall be — shall be forever.

"Do you want anything else?"

Orgilus said, "I would possess my wife; the equity of reason itself bids me. Natural justice based on reason itself tells me that this is permitted."

Possession of his wife would include sleeping with her.

Penthea asked, "Is that all that tells you this is permitted?"

Orgilus replied, "Why, it is the all of me; it is myself that tells me that this is permitted."

Penthea said, "Back away some steps from me. Put some distance between you and me."

He backed away from her.

She then said, "With this space between us, I dare to say a few words, but first put on your disguise."

Orgilus put on his disguise as a scholar and said, "You are obeyed; it is done."

Penthea said, "The heavens witness how, Orgilus, by promise I was yours. The heavens can witness, too, a rape done on my truth."

To Penthea, her marriage was like a rape.

She continued, "How I do love you still, Orgilus, and will continue to love you, must best appear in my giving you your freedom; for I find the constant preservation of your merit, by your not daring to attack my honor and reputation with any indecent amorous proposal, which might give deeper wounds to discontents."

She recognized that Orgilus was a good person, and for him to continue to be a good person, he must give her up. If he were to attempt to have an affair with her — a legally married woman — his goodness would cease to exist, and the affair would lead to much unhappiness, including a bad reputation and deeper unhappiness for her.

She said, "Continue this fair course of action; continue to be good. Do that, and then, although I cannot add to your comfort and happiness, yet I shall more often remember from what fortune I have fallen, and pity my own ruin. I will remember what I have lost, and I will pity myself.

"Live, live happy, happy in your next choice of a wife, so that you may people this virtue-barren age with virtues in your children! Get married to a good wife, and raise good children.

"And oh, when you are married, think about me with mercy, not contempt! I hope that your wife, hearing my story, will not scorn my fall.

"Now let us part from each other."

The disguised Orgilus said, "Part! Yet I will advise you better. This is the truth: Penthea is the wife to Orgilus, and forever Penthea shall be Orgilus' wife."

Penthea said, "Never shall nor will she be Orgilus' wife."

Orgilus said, "What!"

Penthea said, "Listen to me; in a few words I'll tell you why I will never be your wife. The virgin-dowry that my birth bestowed on me has been ravished by another."

Her husband, Bassanes, had taken her virginity.

She continued, "My true love for you, Orgilus, hates to think that Orgilus deserves nothing better than a second bed."

Because she was no longer a virgin, she did not think that she was worthy of becoming the wife of Orgilus.

The disguised Orgilus said, "I must not accept this reason."

Penthea said, "To confirm it: Should I outlive my bondage of marriage to Bassanes, I say let me meet another bondage worse than this and less desired, if, of all men alive, you should only touch my lip or hand again!"

The disguised Orgilus said, "Penthea, now I tell you, you grow reckless in my suffering. You are recklessly making me suffer. Come, sweetheart, you are mine."

Penthea said, "Uncivilized sir, stop this! Or I can turn affection into vengeance. Your reputation, if you value any, lies bleeding at my feet. Unworthy man, if you ever henceforth appear in language, message, or letter, and try to betray my frailty, I'll call your former protestations of love lust, and curse my stars for taking away my judgment.

"Go, you are fit only for disguise and covered walks that will hide your shame. For this once I will spare your life.

"I laugh at my own confidence — the confidence I had in you. Because of your bad behavior, my sorrows are made inferior to my bad fortunes. I do not feel sorrow as much as I did before. Previously, I sorrowed over you, but because of your bad behavior, now I do not. If ever you harbor a worthy love for me, do not dare to answer me. May my good genius — my guardian angel — guide me so that I may never see you again!

"Go away from me!"

Orgilus said, "I'll tear my veil of cunning dissimulation off — I will abandon my disguise, and I will stand up like a man resolved to take action. Action, not words, shall show what kind of man I am.

"Oh, Penthea!"

He exited.

Penthea said to herself, "He sighed my name, I am sure, as he departed from me. I fear I was too rough. Alas, poor gentleman, you looked not like the ruins of your youth, but like the ruins of those ruins.

"Honor — how much we fight against weakness to preserve you!"

Penthea did love Orgilus. She had put on an act to convince him to stay away from her. This was a safeguard for her honor and reputation — she would remain faithful to a husband whom she did not love.

Bassanes and Grausis walked close to her.

Bassanes said to Grausis, "Bah! Damn you, rotten maggot, damn you! Sleep? Sleep at court? Now? May aches, convulsions, abscesses, rheums, gouts, and palsies clog your bones for a dozen more years!"

Grausis said, "Now you are in a bad mood."

Seeing Penthea, Bassanes said, "She's by herself, there's hope of that; she's serious, too. She's in strong contemplation, yes, and composed. The signs are wholesome."

"Very wholesome, truly," Grausis said.

"Hold your jaws, nightmare!" Bassanes said.

He then said to Penthea, "Lady, come. Your brother has been carried to his private room; you must go there."

"Is he not well, my lord?" Penthea asked.

"He has had a sudden fit," Bassanes said. "It will off! It's some surfeit or disorder."

"It will off!" is true. The illness will leave, but 1) the illness could leave the sick person dead, or 2) the illness could leave and the sick person would recover.

Bassanes asked, "How are you, dearest?"

Penthea said, "Your news is not the best."

Prophilus arrived and said to Penthea, "The chief of men, the most excellent Ithocles, desires your presence, madam."

"We are hastening to him," Bassanes said.

Penthea said, "In vain we labor in this course of life to piece our journey out at length, or crave respite of breath: Our home is in the grave."

"Perfect philosophy!" Bassanes said.

Penthea said, "So then let us take care to live so that our reckonings may fall even when we're to make account."

To keep good accounting books, the credit and debit of each transaction must equal each other. We must keep good books so that we are ready for Judgment Day.

This, however, is not the kind of image we expect to hear. Normally, we want the account of our good deeds to be much greater than the account of our bad deeds.

Prophilus said, "He cannot fear who builds on noble grounds: Sickness or pain is the testing-ground undergone by a virtuous person, and your virtuous brother is known as such a person to the world.

"Speak comfort to him, lady; be entirely gentle. Stars fall only in the grossness of our sight. When a good man dies, all the earth loses a light."

The death of a good man is much more important than the fall of a star.

CHAPTER 3
— 3.1 —

Tecnicus and Orgilus were speaking together in Tecnicus' study. Orgilus was not disguised.

"Be well advised," Tecnicus said. "Don't let a resolution of giddy rashness choke the breath of reason."

"It shall not, most sage master," Orgilus said.

"I am suspicious," Tecnicus said, "for if the borrowed shape — the disguise — you so recently put on inferred a purpose, we must conclude that some violent design of a sudden nature has shaken off that shadow, aka disguise, so that now you will fly upon a newly hatched enterprise.

"Orgilus, take heed that you have not, under the cover of my integrity, shrouded unlawful plots. My mortal eyes cannot pierce the secrets of your heart; only the gods know the secrets of people's hearts."

"Learned Tecnicus," Orgilus said, "such suspicions are without a cause, and to clear the truth from misunderstanding, the present state of affairs makes me act this way.

"The Prince of Argos comes himself in person in quest of great Calantha for his bride; she is our kingdom's heir. Besides, my only sister, Euphrania, is betrothed to Prophilus. Lastly, the king is sending letters to Athens for me, demanding my quick return to court. Please accept these reasons for the change in my actions."

Tecnicus said, "These reasons are just ones, Orgilus, and they are not to be contradicted. Yet beware of an unsure foundation; no pretty flags can fortify a building that has weak joints.

"I have observed a growth in your aspect — horoscope and face — of a dangerous extent, sudden, and — look to it — I might add, certain —"

"My aspect!" Orgilus interrupted. "Even if a skillful person could run through my inmost thoughts, he would not sift an inclination there more than what is suited with the justice of my honor."

"I believe it," Tecnicus said, "but know then, Orgilus, what honor is. Honor does not exist in a bare opinion; it is not gotten by doing any act that feeds one's own satisfaction — do not confuse self-satisfaction with honor. Such false honor is splendid in appearance, because we think it is splendid. Such false honor comes by accident, not by nature. Such false honor proceeds from the vices of our passion, which makes our reason drunk.

"Instead, real honor is the reward of virtue, and it is acquired by justice, or by valor that for its basis has justice to uphold it.

"A man fails in honor when for money or revenge he commits thefts, murders, treasons, adulteries, and suchlike by infringing and encroaching on just laws, whose sovereignty is best preserved by justice. Crimes committed in the name of honor are not honorable.

"Thus you see how honor must be grounded on knowledge, not opinion — for opinion relies on probability and accident, but knowledge relies on necessity and truth.

"I leave you to the fit consideration of what becomes the grace of real honor.

"I wish success to all your virtuous intentions."

Orgilus said, "May the gods increase your wisdom, reverend oracle, and may the gods in your precepts make me ever prosperous!"

Tecnicus said, "I thank you for your wish."

Orgilus exited.

Tecnicus said to himself about Orgilus, "Much mystery of fate lies hidden in that man's fortunes; ingenuity of mind may lead his actions to splendid undertakings — but let the gods be rulers still: No human power can forestall their will."

Armostes entered the study, carrying a box.

Tecnicus asked, "From where have you come?"

"From the presence of King Amyclas," Armostes said. "Pardon my interruption of your studies.

"Here, in this sealed box, he sends a treasure to you, a treasure as dear to him as his crown. He requests that your grave person would examine, ponder, sift, and double-sift the pith and circumstance of every tittle that the scroll inside the box contains."

"What is the scroll, Armostes?" Tecnicus asked.

Armostes replied, "It is the health of Sparta, the king's life, the muscles and safety of the commonwealth. It is the sum of what the oracle delivered when the king last visited the prophetic temple at Delphi.

"What the king's reasons are for why, after so long a silence, he requires your counsel now, grave man, his majesty himself will soon acquaint you with."

Tecnicus took the box and prayed, "Apollo, inspire my intellect!"

Apollo is the god of prophecy.

Tecnicus asked, "Has the Prince of Argos been welcomed?"

"He has," Armostes replied, "and he has requested our princess for his wife, which I believe to be one special cause why the king importunes you for an interpretation of the oracle."

Tecnicus said, "My duty to the king, good peace to Sparta, and fair day to Armostes!"

Armostes said, "Likewise to Tecnicus!"

In Ithocles' apartment in the palace, soft music played. Prophilus and Penthea were by Ithocles, who was sleeping in bed. Bassanes and Grausis entered quietly and listened to this song that was being sung for Ithocles:

"Can you paint a thought? Or number
"Every fancy in a slumber?
"Can you count soft minutes roving
"From a dial's point by moving?
"Can you grasp a sigh? Or, lastly,
"Rob a virgin's honor chastely?
"No, oh, no! Yet you may
"Sooner do both that and this,
"This and that, and never miss,
"Than by any praise display
"Beauty's beauty; such a glory,
"As beyond all fate, all story,
"All arms, all arts,
"All loves, all hearts,
"Greater than those or they,
"Do, shall, and must obey. "

Bassanes said, "All is silent, calm, secure. Grausis, no creaking? No noise? Do you hear anything?"

Grausis replied, "Not a mouse, or whisper of the wind."

"The floor is covered with mats," Bassanes said. "The bedposts surely are steel or marble. Soldiers should not like, I think, songs that are so effeminate. Sounds of such delicacy are but fawnings upon the sloth of lechery; they heighten cinders of covert lust up to a flame."

"What do you mean, my lord?" Grausis said. "Speak low; that gabbling of yours will do nothing but ruin us."

Bassanes said, "Chamber-combats are felt, not heard."

Chamber-combats are amorous encounters in bed.

Prophilus said, "Ithocles is awakening."

"What's that?" Bassanes said softly.

Ithocles said, "Who's there? Sister? Everyone else leave the room."

Bassanes said, "It is consented!"

Bassanes was so jealous that he thought that Ithocles and Penthea were going to commit incest.

Prophilus said, "Lord Bassanes, your brother-in-law wants to have some privacy. We must allow him that; he has just awakened. Please withdraw from the bedchamber."

"Of course," Bassanes said, "it is a fitting request."

Prophilus said to Grausis, "Gentlewoman, leave, too."

"Yes, I will, sir," Grausis said.

Prophilus, Bassanes, and Grausis exited.

Ithocles and Penthea were now alone.

"Sit nearer, sister, to me," Ithocles said.

She sat nearer, but he said, "Nearer still."

She moved closer, and he said, "We had one father, in one womb we took life, we twins were brought up together, yet we have lived at a distance, like two strangers.

"I could wish that the first pillow on which I was cradled had proven to be a grave for me. I wish that I had died when I was a baby."

Penthea said, "If you had died as a baby, then you would have been happy. Then you would never have known that sin of life that blots all following glories with a vengeance, as a result of your forfeiting the last will of the dead man from whom you had your being."

Their late father was Thrasus, and his last will was that Penthea be married to Orgilus, but Ithocles had gone against their father's last will and made Penthea marry the jealous Bassanes.

"Sad Penthea, you cannot be too cruel," Ithocles said. "My rash spleen has with a violent hand plucked from your bosom a lover-blessed heart, to grind it into dust, for which my heart is now breaking."

Penthea said, "Not yet, heaven, I beg you! First let some wild fires scorch, but not consume it! May the heat be cherished with infinite desires, but impossible hopes!"

Ithocles said, "Wronged soul, your prayers are heard. I suffer in that way — I have infinite desires, but impossible hopes."

Penthea said, "Here, lo, I breathe, a miserable creature, led to ruin by an unnatural brother — a brother who did not act brotherly to me!"

Ithocles said, "I consume in languishing affections — in grief — for that trespass, yet I cannot die."

Penthea said, "A country girl who works for wages drinks the untroubled streams with leaping kids and with the bleating lambs, and so allays her thirst secure and free from anxiety, while I quench my hot sighs with streams of my tears."

Ithocles said, "The laborer eats his coarsest bread, earned with his sweat, and lies down to sleep, while every bit of food I touch turns during digestion into gall as bitter as Penthea's curse. Give me any penance, any punishment, for my tyranny, and I will call you merciful."

Penthea said, "Please kill me. Rid me from living with a jealous husband, and then we will join in friendship, and be again brother and sister. Kill me, please. Will you?"

Ithocles asked, "How does your husband regard and esteem you?"

Penthea said, "As such a one as only you have made me: as a faith-breaker and sin-spotted whore. Forgive me. I am a sin-spotted whore in act, but not in desires, as the gods must witness."

Ithocles had made her a faith-breaker by making her marry Bassanes, instead of Orgilus, to whom she had been betrothed. Because she slept with Bassanes, Penthea regarded herself as a sin-spotted whore.

Ithocles said, "You belie and misrepresent your friend."

Which friend? Orgilus? Bassanes? Or Ithocles himself? Or Penthea perhaps, if she is supposed to be a friend to herself?

Penthea replied, "I do not, Ithocles, for she who is wife to Orgilus, and lives in known adultery with Bassanes, is at the best a whore.

"Will you kill me now?

"The cremated ashes of our parents will assume some dreadful figure, and appear to charge you with your bloody guilt that has betrayed their name to infamy in this reproachful match."

Ithocles said, "After my victories abroad, at home I meet despair; ingratitude of nature has made my actions monstrous.

"You shall stand as a deity, my sister, and be worshipped for your resolved martyrdom; wronged maidens and married wives shall to your hallowed shrine offer their prayers, and crowned with myrtle, which is sacred to Venus, goddess of love, they shall sacrifice pure and faithful turtledoves.

"Yes, you shall stand as a deity if you can pity a brother who is bending under pressure and lend just one finger to ease that pressure."

Penthea said, "Oh, no more!"

Ithocles said, "Death waits to waft me to the banks of the river Styx in Hell and free me from this chaos of my bondage, and until you will forgive me, I must endure."

Ithocles had not mentioned being in love, but his newfound empathy for Penthea and his suffering infinite desires and impossible hopes had convinced her that he must be in love.

Penthea asked, "Who is the saint you serve?"

By "saint you serve," she meant, "woman you love."

Ithocles said, "Friendship, or nearness of birth to any but my sister, dared not have asked that question; it is a secret, sister, that I dare not murmur to myself."

Penthea said, "Let me — by your new protestations to me I conjure you — learn her name."

Ithocles said, "Her name? ... It is ... it is ... I dare not tell you."

Penthea said, "All your protestations of respect for me are forged. You do not care for me, despite what you said."

Ithocles said, "They are not forged. Peace! The saint is ... Calantha ... the princess ... the king's daughter ... sole heir of Sparta. Me, I am most miserable. Do you know I love you now that I have told you the name of the saint I serve?

"For my injuries against you, revenge yourself with bravery, and speak my treasons into the king's ears — do it."

Although he was a Spartan military hero, Ithocles was not of a high enough class to marry Calantha, daughter of the King of Sparta.

Ithocles continued, "Calantha does not yet know I love her, nor does Prophilus, my closest friend."

Penthea said, "Suppose you were contractually engaged to marry her, would it not split even your very soul to see her father snatch her out of your arms against her will, and force her to marry the Prince of Argos?"

Ithocles said, "Don't trouble the fountains of my eyes with your own story; I sweat blood for it."

Anyone who metaphorically sweats drops of blood feels the deepest sorrow.

Penthea said, "We are reconciled. I forgive you. Alas, sir, being children, the only two branches of one stock, it is not fitting that we should divide. Have comfort, you may find it."

Ithocles said, "Yes, in you; only in you, my Penthea."

Penthea said, "If sorrows have not too much dulled my infected brain, I'll attempt to devise a plan of action."

Ithocles said, "Mad man! Why have I wronged a maiden who is so excellent!"

Ithocles was the mad man, and Penthea was the maiden.

Bassanes, Prophilus, Groneas, Hemophil, and Grausis all entered Ithocles' chamber.

Bassanes, who was carrying a dagger, said, "I can restrain myself no longer, and I will restrain myself no longer."

Ithocles stood up. This was an emergency.

The others tried to restrain Bassanes, who said, "Keep your hands away from me, or fall upon the point of my dagger. My patience is tired because like a slow-paced ass, you ride my easy nature, and proclaim my slothful approach to vengeance a reproach and a personal characteristic of mine."

"What is the meaning of this rudeness?" Ithocles asked.

"He's insane," Prophilus said.

"Oh, my aggrieved lord!" Penthea said to Bassanes, her lord and husband.

"Sweet lady, don't come near him," Grausis said. "He holds his perilous weapon in his hand to prick he cares not whom nor where — see, see, see!"

She was unconsciously bawdy with her use of the terms "weapon" and "prick."

"My birth is noble," Bassanes said to Ithocles. "Though the popular blast of vanity, as giddy as your youth, has reared your name up to bestride a cloud, or progress in the chariot of the sun, I am no clod of trade, to be a lackey to pride."

He was saying that Ithocles' military success and public acclaim had made the young man vain — as vain as two other young men. Ixion, a mortal, fell in love with the goddess Juno and wanted to seduce her. Jupiter, Juno's husband, tricked Ixion by shaping a cloud to resemble Juno. Ixion had sex with the cloud, and from that union was born Centauros, who mated with mares and created the first Centaurs, who are half-human, half-horse creatures. The other young man was Phaëton, a mortal who attempted to drive the sun-chariot across the sky. Being mortal, he couldn't control the immortal horses that drew the sun-chariot. Jupiter killed Phaëton with a thunderbolt before the out-of-control sun-chariot destroyed the Earth.

Bassanes continued, "Nor am I like your attendant slave, waiting outside the bawdy hinges of your doors while you have sex inside, or whistling to notify you of secret communications such as letters of assignation or whistling to notify you of the arrival of women relevant to your bed-sports."

The courtier Groneas said, "These are fine moods! They become him."

The courtier Hemophil said, "How he stares, struts, puffs, and sweats! Most remarkable lunacy!"

Ithocles said, "Except that I may conceive that the spirit of wine has taken possession of your soberer self, I'd say you were unmannerly."

Bassanes said to Ithocles, "Unmannerly!"

"Dear brother!" Penthea said.

He contemptuously said to Penthea, his wife, "Meow, kitten!"

He then said to Ithocles, "Smooth Formality is usher to the rankness of the blood, but Impudence bears up the train. Indeed, sir, your fiery mettle, or your youthful blaze of huge renown, is not sufficient warrant to print upon my forehead the scornful word 'cuckold.'"

"His jealousy has robbed him of his wits," Ithocles said. "He doesn't know what he is saying."

Bassanes replied, "Yes, and he knows to whom he talks: to one who fattens — as one fattens swine — his lust in the swine-security of bestial incest."

"Ha, devil!" Ithocles said.

Bassanes said, "I will halloo your incest and proclaim it to everyone although I blush more to name the filthiness than you blush to act it."

"Monster!" Ithocles said, drawing his sword.

Prophilus said, "Sir, by our friendship —"

Penthea said, "By our bloods —"

She then asked, "Will you quite ruin us both, brother?"

A bloody quarrel with Bassanes would ruin any chance Ithocles had of marrying Calantha.

Grausis said about Bassanes, "Damn him! These are his whims, caprices, and melancholies."

Hemophil said to her, "Well said, old touch-hole."

"Touch-hole" has a bawdy meaning, in addition to being the name of the hole in early firearms through which gunpowder is ignited.

Groneas said, "Kick him out of doors."

Penthea said, "With your permission, let me speak."

She then said to Bassanes, "My lord, what slackness in my obedience to you has deserved this rage? Unless my humility and silent duty have drawn on your troubledness, my simplicity has never deliberately attempted to cause you vexation."

Bassanes replied, "Light of beauty, deal not ungently with a desperate wound! No breach of reason dares make war with her whose looks are sovereignty, whose breath is balm. Oh, that I could preserve you in the pleasures of possession as in devotion!"

Penthea said, "Sir, may every evil locked in Pandora's box shower, in your presence, on my unhappy head, if, since you made me a partner in your bed, I have been faulty and guilty of even one unseemly thought against your honor!"

After Prometheus stole fire from the gods and gave it to human beings, Zeus, king of the gods, got revenge. He gave the mortal woman Pandora to be the wife of Epimetheus, the brother of Prometheus. Zeus gave Pandora a box, but he warned her never to open it. Curious, Pandora opened the box, and evils such as death and disease poured out of the box.

Ithocles said, "Don't purge his griefs, Penthea. Let him suffer."

Bassanes said to Penthea, "Yes, speak on, excellent creature!"

To Ithocles, he said, "Good sir, don't be a hindrance to peace and the praise of virtue. Oh, my senses are charmed with celestial sounds!"

Bassanes now believed that Penthea was now and had been a faithful wife.

He said to Penthea, "Speak on, dear, speak on. I never gave you one ill word. Answer. Did I? Indeed, I did not."

Penthea replied, "Nor, by the forehead of Juno, goddess of marriage, was I ever guilty of a wanton error."

"A goddess!" Bassanes said. "Let me kneel before you!"

Grausis said, "Alas, kind animal!"

Ithocles said, "No, but you may kneel for penance."

Bassanes said, "Noble sir, what penance is it? With gladness I embrace it, yet please don't let my rashness teach you to be too unmerciful."

Ithocles replied, "When you shall show good proof that manly wisdom, not overswayed by strong emotion or opinion, knows how to lead your judgment, then this lady — your wife, my sister — shall return in safety home, to be guided by you, but until I can from clear evidence certify it first, she shall be in my care. Until you can control yourself, my sister will stay with me."

Bassanes said, "Rip my bosom up, and I'll stand the ripping steadfastly. This torture of being separated from my wife is unendurable."

Ithocles replied, "Well, sir, I dare not trust her to your fury."

Bassanes said, "But Penthea does not say that."

Penthea said, "She needs no tongue to plead an excuse who never offered wrong."

Hemophil said sarcastically to Grausis, "Virgin of reverence and antiquity, you stay behind. Don't go with us."

"The court does not want your diligence," Groneas said to Grausis, "The court does not want you around."

Everyone exited except Bassanes and Grausis.

"What will you do, my lord?" Grausis said. "Penthea, the lady I serve, is gone; I am forbidden to follow her."

Bassanes asked, "May I see her, or speak to her once more sometime?"

Grausis said, "And feel her, too, man. Be of good cheer, she's your own flesh and bone. When you married her, you became one."

Bassanes said, "Desperate diseases must find desperate cures. She swore that she has been true to me."

Grausis said, "And she said the truth, I swear on my modesty."

Bassanes said, "Let him not be believed who does not give credit to the vows she made! Much wrong I did to her, but to her brother I did infinite wrong. Rumor will call me the contempt of manhood should I run on like this. Somehow I must try to outdo what I have made myself, and cry out against jealousy."

In a room in the palace, Amyclas, King of Sparta, was entertaining Nearchus, Prince of Argos. Others present included Calantha, Armostes, Crotolon, Euphrania, Chrystalla, Philema, and Amelus.

Using the royal plural, King Amyclas said to Nearchus, "Cousin of Argos, what the heavens have pleased, in their unchanging counsels to conclude for both our kingdoms' prosperity and welfare, we must submit to. Nor can we be unthankful to the bounties of the gods, who, when we were so old that we were even creeping to our grave, sent us a daughter, in whose birth continues our hope of succession.

"As you are next in line to become King of Sparta, being grandchild to our aunt, so we in our heart desire that you may sit nearest Calantha's love, since we have always vowed not to enforce affection by our will, but by her own choice to confirm it gladly. We hope that Calantha will love you of her own free will."

Nearchus replied, "Your speech reveals the nature of a very just father. I did not come here to roughly demand my cousin's thralldom, but instead to free my own thralldom of love by marrying Calantha. Reports of great Calantha's beauty, virtue, sweetness, and singular perfections courted all ears to believe what I find was published by constant truth, from which, if any meritorious service on my part can purchase a fair interpretation of me, this lady must command it."

Nearchus was Calantha's second cousin, and he was King Amyclas' first cousin, once removed.

Calantha replied, "Princely sir, so well you know how to profess courtship that you instruct your hearers to become practitioners in homage, of which number I'll study to be the chief practitioner."

Nearchus said, "You are chief, glorious virgin, in my devotions, as in all men's wonder."

King Amyclas said, "Excellent cousin, we deny you no liberty. Use your own opportunities."

He meant that he would give Nearchus opportunities to talk to Calantha.

King Amyclas then said, "Armostes, we must consult with the philosophers: The business is of importance."

Armostes said, "Sir, at your pleasure."

Nearchus and Calantha spoke together while King Amyclas, Armostes, and Crotolon met.

King Amyclas said, "You told me, Crotolon, that your son has returned from Athens. Why then hasn't he come to court as we commanded?"

Crotolon replied, "He shall soon wait on your royal will, great sir."

King Amyclas said, "The marriage between young Prophilus and Euphrania tastes of too much delay."

Crotolon began, "My lord —"

King Amyclas interrupted, "Some pleasures during the celebration of the marriage would give life to the entertainment of the prince our kinsman. Our court wears gravity more than we relish."

Armostes said, "Yet the heavens smile without a cloud on all your noble enterprises."

"So may the gods protect us," Crotolon said.

A short distance from the others, Calantha said to Nearchus, "A prince a subject?"

Nearchus said, "Yes, a subject to beauty's scepter. Just as all hearts kneel to you, so do mine."

Calantha said, "You are too courtly."

Ithocles and Prophilus entered the room, and then Orgilus arrived.

Ithocles said to Orgilus, "Your safe return to Sparta is very welcome. I rejoice to meet you here, and as occasion shall grant us privacy, I will yield you reasons why I should covet to deserve the title and position of being your respected friend, for without courtly flattery, believe it, Orgilus, being your friend is my ambition."

Orgilus replied, "Your lordship may command me, your poor servant."

Seeing Nearchus and Calantha talking so closely together, Ithocles thought, *So amorously close! So soon! My heart!*

Looking at Ithocles, Prophilus thought, *What sudden change is next?*

He had been worried about Ithocles ever since Ithocles had returned to Sparta after achieving military victory.

Ithocles said, "Life to the king, to whom I here present this noble gentleman, newly come from Athens. Royal sir, vouchsafe your gracious hand in favor of his merit."

The king gave Orgilus his hand to kiss.

Crotolon thought, *My son preferred by Ithocles!*

This was a big deal. King Amyclas and Ithocles were showing respect to Orgilus. Ithocles had recommended Orgilus to the king, and he wanted the king to show respect and give bounty to Orgilus.

King Amyclas said, "Our bounties shall open to you, Orgilus; for instance — listen closely with your ear — if, out of those literary compositions that flow and are abundant in Athens, you have there acquired some rarity of wit to grace the nuptials of your fair sister, and make famous our court in the eyes of this young Prince Nearchus, we shall be debtor to your act of inventive literary imagination. Think on it."

"Your highness honors me," Orgilus replied.

Nearchus said to Calantha, "My tongue and heart are twins."

Calantha replied, "A noble birth, and one becoming such a father."

Calantha then said, "Worthy Orgilus, you are a guest most wished for."

Orgilus replied, "May my duty always rise in your opinion, sacred Princess!"

Ithocles said to Nearchus, "This is Euphrania's brother, sir; he is a gentleman who is well worth your knowing."

Using the majestic plural, Nearchus replied, "We embrace him, and we are proud of so dear and valuable an acquaintance."

King Amyclas said, "All prepare for revels and entertainment; the joys of Hymen, like Phoebus the sun-god in his luster, put to flight all mists of dullness and crown the hours with gladness. Let there be no sounds but music, and no discourse but mirth!"

Calantha requested, "Give me your arm, please, Ithocles."

Nearchus offered her his arm, but Calantha said, "No, my good Lord, keep on your way; I am provided with an arm."

Nearchus said, "I dare not disobey."

Ithocles said, "Most heavenly lady!"

Crotolon and Orgilus spoke together in a room in Crotolon's house.

Crotolon said, "The king has spoken his mind about marriage between Prophilus and Euphrania."

Orgilus said, "His will he has, but if it were lawful to try a legal action against the power of greatness, not the reason, perhaps such undershrubs as subjects sometimes might draw on natural justice to guide the authority a king holds without check over a meek obedience."

Crotolon asked, "What are your thoughts about your sister's marriage? Prophilus is a deserving, promising youth."

Orgilus said, "I don't envy his merit, but instead I applaud it. I could wish him prosperity in all his best desires and with a willingness enleague — unite — our blood with his through marriage, for the purchase of full growth in friendship. He never touched on any wrong that threatened to harm the honor of our house nor disturbed our peace. Yet, with your permission, let me not forget under whose wing he gathers warmth and comfort, whose creature he is bound, made, and must live so."

Orgilus meant that Prophilus was the close friend of Ithocles, who had taken Penthea from Orgilus and given her to Bassanes.

Crotolon said, "Son, son, I find in you a harsh disposition. No courtesy can win it; it is too rancorous."

Orgilus replied, "Good sir, don't be severe in your interpretation. I am no stranger to such easy calms as sit in tender bosoms. Lordly Ithocles has graced my entertainment in abundance by making a recommendation of me to the king. Ithocles has descended very humbly from that height of arrogance and anger that wrought the rape on aggrieved Penthea's purity; his scorn of my unprosperous fortunes is reclaimed and is now a courtship, almost a fawning — I'll kiss his foot, since you will have it so."

"Since I will have it so!" Crotolon said. "Friend, I will have it so, without our ruin and destruction by your cunning plots, or the wolf of hatred snarling in your breast. You have a spirit, sir, have you? A familiar spirit that rides in the air to give you information? Some such hobgoblin hurried you from Athens because you came here unsent for."

Orgilus had returned to Sparta before letters ordering him to return reached Athens, where people supposed him to be staying. Of course, he had overheard Prophilus talking about having him recalled from Athens.

Orgilus said, "If I am unwelcome here, I might have found a grave there."

Crotolon said, "Surely, your business was soon dispatched, or else you changed your mind quickly."

Orgilus lied, "It was concern, sir, about my health that cut short my journey because in Athens a general plague threatens to make the city a desolation."

Crotolon said, "And I fear that you brought back a worse infection with you — infection of your mind, which, as you say, threatens the desolation of our family."

"Forbid it, our dear genius! May the protecting spirit of our family forbid it!" Orgilus said.

Orgilus continued, "I would rather be made a sacrifice on Thrasus' monument, or kneel to Ithocles, his son, in the dust than woo a father's curse. My sister's marriage with Prophilus is from my heart confirmed and assented to. May I live hated and may I die despised if I omit to further that marriage in all that can concern me!"

"I have been too rough," Crotolon apologized. "My duty to my king made me so earnest that I have been too rough. Excuse my words, Orgilus."

Orgilus began, "Dear sir —"

Crotolon interrupted, "Here comes Euphrania with Prophilus and Ithocles."

Prophilus, Euphrania, and Ithocles entered the room. With them were the courtiers Groneas and Hemophil.

Orgilus said to Ithocles, "Most honored! Ever famous!"

Ithocles was honoring Orgilus and his father by visiting them.

"I am your true friend," Ithocles said. "On earth you do not have any truer friend.

"With benign eyes look on this worthy couple; your consent can alone make them one."

"They have my consent," Orgilus said. "Sister, you pledged to me an oath, from which engagement I never will release you, if you aim at any other choice than this. I will agree to have you marry no one other than Prophilus."

Euphrania said, "Dear brother, I aim to marry him, or no one."

Crotolon said, "To Orgilus' blessing, my blessing is added."

Orgilus now led the betrothal ceremony, saying, "Until a greater ceremony — marriage — perfects your relationship, Euphrania, give me your hand.

"Here, take her hand, Prophilus.

"Live long as a happy man and wife.

"Further, so that these people present may infer an omen, I sing this as a bridal song as I close my wishes:

"*Comforts lasting, loves increasing,*

"*Like soft hours never ceasing:*

"*Plenty's pleasure, peace complying,*

"*Without jars [quarrels], or tongues envying [malicious tongues];*

"*Hearts by holy union wedded,*

"*More than theirs by custom bedded;*

"*Fruitful issues; life so graced,*

"*Not by age to be defaced,*

"*Budding, as the year ensues,*

"*Every spring another youth [Every spring a boy is born to you]:*

"*All what thought can add beside*

"*Crown this bridegroom and this bride!*"

Prophilus said, "You have sealed joy close to my soul."

He added, "Euphrania, now I may call you mine."

Ithocles said, "I am only exchanging one good friend for another."

He was losing Prophilus to Euphrania, but he thought he was gaining Orgilus as a friend.

Orgilus said, "If these gallants will please to grace a poor literary invention by joining with me in some slight device, I'll venture on a literary effort my younger days have studied for delight."

The word "device" was a pun that meant 1) dramatic presentation such as a play, and 2) cunning and underhanded stratagem.

Hemophil said, "With thankful willingness, I offer my attendance."

Groneas said, "No endeavor of mine shall fail to show itself."

Ithocles said, "We will all join to wait on your directions, Orgilus."

Orgilus said, "Oh, my good lord, your favors flow towards a too unworthy worm — but as you please. I am what you will shape me to be."

Ithocles said, "Then you are a fast friend."

Crotolon said, "I thank you, son, for this acknowledgment. It is a sight of gladness."

Orgilus replied, "It is only my duty."

In Calantha's apartment in the palace, Calantha and Penthea were speaking. Also present were Chrystalla and Philema, two female attendants who served Calantha.

Calantha ordered Chrystalla and Philema, "If anyone should want to speak with us, refuse him entrance. Be careful to obey this order."

"We shall, madam," Chrystalla said.

"Except for the king himself," Calantha said, "give no one admittance — not anyone."

Philema said, "Madam, we shall take care to obey your order."

Chrystalla and Philema exited.

Calantha said, "Being alone, Penthea, you have been granted the opportunity you sought, and might at all times have commanded."

Penthea said, "It is a benefit that I shall owe your goodness even in death for. My hourglass of life, sweet princess, has few minutes remaining to run down; the sands of the hourglass are spent, for by an inward messenger I feel the summons for my departure from life to be soon and certain."

"You feel too much your melancholy," Calantha said.

Penthea said, "Glories of human greatness are only pleasing dreams and shadows soon decaying. On the stage of my mortality, my youth has acted some scenes of vanity, drawn out at length by varied pleasures, sweetened in the mixture, but tragic in the conclusion. Beauty, pomp, along with every sensual pleasure of the senses that our giddy changeableness frames an idol, are inconstant friends, when any troubled passion makes assault on the unguarded castle of the mind."

Calantha said, "Don't condemn your condition in life because of the 'proof' of bare opinion only. For what purpose have you brought out all these moral texts?"

Penthea replied, "To place before you a perfect mirror, wherein you may see how weary I am of a lingering life. I count the best life as a misery."

"Indeed," Calantha said, "you have no little cause for doing so, yet you have no cause so great as to despair of ever having a remedy."

Penthea said, "That remedy must be a winding-sheet, a coffin of lead, and some unwalked-on corner in the earth. Not to detain your expectation, princess, but I have a humble petition to make to you."

Calantha said, "Speak. I urge you to make it."

Penthea said, "Vouchsafe, then, to be my executrix, and take that trouble on you to dispose such legacies as I bequeath, impartially. I have not much to give, and so the pains you will need to take are easy. Heaven will reward your piety and thank you for it when I am dead, for surely I must not live. I hope that I cannot live."

Calantha said, "Now, curse your sadness. You make me too much woman."

She wept.

Penthea thought, *Her fair eyes melt into passion.*

She said out loud, "Then I have assurance encouraging my boldness. In this paper my will is written down. The contents of my will, you — with your permission — shall now know from my own mouth."

Calantha said, "Talk on, please; this is a pretty foretaste of what is to come."

Penthea said, "I have left to me only three poor jewels to bequeath. The first is my youth, for although I am very old in griefs, in years I am still a child."

Calantha asked, "To whom do you bequeath that jewel?"

Penthea answered, "To virgin-wives, such as those who don't abuse wedlock with freedom of desires, but instead covet chiefly the pledges of chaste beds for ties of love, rather than the ranging of their blood."

"Virgin-wives" are chaste wives. They engage in legitimate sex and bear children who are the pledges of their chaste beds, but they don't have illegitimate sex and allow their blood — passion — to range outside their marriage.

She continued, "And also I leave my youth to married maidens, such as prefer the number of honorable issue in their virtues before the flattery of delights by marriage. May those be forever young!"

"Married maidens" are nuns, who are married to Jesus but who remain virgins and cultivate virtues.

Calantha asked, "Do you mean to part with a second jewel?"

Penthea replied, "My second jewel is my reputation, which I trust is yet untouched by scandal. This I bequeath to Memory, and to Time's old daughter,

Truth. If ever my unhappy name should find mention when I am fallen to dust, may it deserve befitting charity without dishonor!"

A proverb stated, "Truth is the daughter of Time."

Calantha said, "How handsomely you play with the harmless sport of pure imagination! Speak about the last jewel. I strangely like your will."

Penthea said, "This third and final jewel, madam, is dearly precious to me; you must use the best of your discretion to employ this gift as I intend it."

Calantha said, "Do not doubt me. I will employ this gift as you intend it."

Penthea said, "It is long ago since first I lost my heart. Long I have lived without it, or else for certain I should have given that, too; but instead of giving my heart to great Calantha, Sparta's heir, by service bound and by affection vowed, I bequeath my heart, in the holiest rites of love, to my only brother, Ithocles."

Calantha asked, "What did you say?"

Penthea said, "Impute not, heaven-blest lady, to ambition a faith as humbly perfect as the prayers of a devoted suppliant can endow it. Look on Ithocles, princess, with an eye of pity. How like the ghost of what he recently appeared, he moves before you."

Calantha thought, *Shall I answer here, or lend my ear too indecorously?*

Penthea continued, "His heart shall first fall in cinders, scorched by your disdain, before he will dare, poor man, to open an eye on these divine looks, but with low-bent thoughts accusing such presumption. He is afraid to look at you with an expression that would reveal that he loves you.

"As for words, he dares not utter any except words of service, yet this lost creature loves you although he is afraid to tell you that.

"Be a princess in sweetness as in blood; give him his doom, or raise him up to comfort."

Calantha asked, "What new change appears in my behavior, that you dare to tempt my displeasure?"

Penthea said, "I must leave the world to revel in Elysium, and it is just and good to wish my brother some advantage here. Yet, I swear by my best hopes of achieving Elysium, Ithocles is ignorant of my approaching you and telling you that he loves you. But if you please to kill him, give him one angry look or one harsh word, and you shall soon conclude how strong a power your absolute authority holds over his life and end."

Calantha said, "You have forgotten, Penthea, that I still have a father."

She meant that her father the king was unlikely to allow her to marry Ithocles.

Penthea replied, "But remember that I am a sister, although to me this brother has been, you know, unkind — oh, very unkind!"

His unkindness had been marrying her to Bassanes rather than to Orgilus.

Calantha said loudly, "Chrystalla, Philema, where are you?"

She then said to Penthea, "Lady, your rebuke lies in my silence."

Chrystalla and Philema entered the room and said, "Madam, here we are."

Calantha said, "I think you sleep, you drones. Wait on Penthea; escort her to her lodging."

She thought, *Ithocles? Wronged lady!*

Calantha actually liked hearing that Ithocles loved her, although she was sure that her father would not approve. She was wronging Penthea by rebuking her.

Penthea said, "My reckonings are made even; death or fate can now neither strike too soon, nor enforce too late."

She meant that she had just done a good deed that would make up for all her bad deeds. She was ready to die.

CHAPTER 4

— 4.1 —

In Ithocles' apartment in the palace, Ithocles and Armostes talked. Armostes, Ithocles' uncle, was worried about Ithocles' friendship with Orgilus.

Ithocles said, "Stop your inquisition. Excessive care has too subtle and too searching a nature. In fears of love and friendship, it is too quick, and too slow of credit. I am not what you suspect me to be."

Armostes said, "Nephew, be then as I would wish. All is not right."

He was worried about Orgilus, who had reason to hate Ithocles.

He then prayed, "May the good heaven confirm your resolutions for dependence on worthy ends, which may advance your quiet!"

His prayer was that Ithocles' decision to be a friend to Orgilus would end well.

Ithocles said, "I did the noble Orgilus much injury, but I grieved Penthea more. I now repent it — now, uncle, now; this 'now' is now too late. So fertile is folly in sad issue, that after-wit, like bankrupts' debts, stands tallied, without all possibilities of payment."

"After-wit" is intelligence and knowledge learned after the fact. We may learn from our mistakes, but the mistakes' consequences remain. Similarly, when a man goes bankrupt, his debtors miss out on repayment.

Ithocles continued, "Surely, Orgilus is an honest, very honest gentleman; he is a man of single, sincere meaning."

A man of single meaning is not an equivocator; he is not a man who says something that can be interpreted in two ways, one good and one bad.

Actually, Orgilus was an equivocator. Earlier, he had spoken about some men joining with him in some slight device. The word "device" was a pun that meant 1) dramatic presentation such as a play, and 2) cunning and underhanded stratagem.

Armostes said, "I believe it. Yet, nephew, it is the tongue that informs our ears. Our eyes can never pierce into the thoughts, for they are lodged too inward. Sometimes, the words a person says do not match their thoughts, but I question no truth in Orgilus —"

Hearing a noise, he looked up and said, "— the Princess Calantha, sir."

Ithocles said, "The princess!"

Armostes added, "Nearchus, the Prince of Argos, is with her."

Nearchus, leading Calantha, and his friend Amelus entered the room. Accompanying them were Chrystalla and Philema. Nearchus and Calantha were equal enough in social class to be married. Nearchus was the Prince of Argos, and Calantha was the Princess of Sparta.

Nearchus said to Calantha, "Great fair one, grace my hopes with any instance of livery, from the allowance of your favor."

The livery was a gift from a woman that the man could wear to show that the woman favored him.

He pointed to a ring on her finger and said, "For example, this little spark."

Calantha said, "It is a toy!"

The word "toy" meant 1) trifle, or 2) plaything.

Picking up on the second meaning, Nearchus replied, "Love feasts on toys, for Cupid, the god of love, is a child. Vouchsafe to give me this bounty: It cannot be denied."

Calantha said, "You shall not value, sweet cousin, at a price, what I account as cheap."

Nearchus and Calantha were second cousins.

She continued, "So cheap, that let him take it who dares stoop for it, and give it at their next meeting to a loved one. She'll thank him for it, perhaps."

She cast the ring in front of Ithocles, who stooped and picked it up.

Amelus, a close friend to Nearchus, said to Ithocles, "The ring, sir, is the princess'; I could have picked it up."

He would have picked it up on behalf of Nearchus and given it to him.

Ithocles replied, "Learn manners, please."

He then said to Calantha, "To the blessed owner, upon my knees."

He knelt and offered the ring to Calantha.

Nearchus said to Ithocles, "You are saucy and insolent."

Calantha said, "This is clever! I am, perhaps, a mistress — a loved woman. This is wondrously clever!

"Let the man keep his fortune, since he found it. He's worthy of it.

"Let's go, cousin!"

Nearchus and Calantha exited.

Ithocles said to Amelus, "Follow them, spaniel, or else I'll force you to a fawning."

The word "spaniel" was an insult.

Amelus replied, "You don't dare to."

Amelus exited, leaving Ithocles and Armostes, Ithocles' uncle, alone.

Armostes said, "My lord, you were too forward."

Ithocles replied, "Look, uncle, there are some such people whose easy satisfactions swarm without care in every sort of plenty, who after full repasts can lay them down to sleep; and they sleep, uncle, and in this silence their very dreams present them with a choice of pleasures. These pleasures — pay attention to me, uncle — are of splendid appearance. Here are heaps of gold, there are increments of honors, now there is change of garments, and then there are the votes of people. Soon appear a variety of beautiful women, courting, in flatteries of the night, an exchange of sexual dalliance in bed, yet these are still only dreams.

"Give me felicity and happiness of which my awoken senses are partakers; give me real, visible, material happiness. And then, too, give me real, visible, material happiness when I am doubtful about expectance of the least comfort that can cherish life — I saw it, sir, I saw it; for it came from her own hand."

Armostes acknowledged, "The princess threw it to you."

Ithocles said, "That is true; and she said — I remember well what she said — her cousin prince would beg it."

Armostes said, "Yes, and he departed in anger because you took it."

Ithocles said to himself, "Penthea, oh, you have pleaded my case to Calantha with a powerful language! I lack the means to adequately reward your merit, but I will do —"

Armostes interrupted, "What is it you are saying?"

Ithocles immediately began talking aloud about something different: "He departed in anger! In anger let him depart; for if his breath, like whirlwinds, could toss such servile slaves as lick the dust his footsteps print into a vapor, it would not dare to stir a hair of mine, it would not; I'd rend my hair out by the roots before I would let that happen. To be anything Calantha smiles on is to be a blessing more sacred than a petty prince of Argos can wish to equal, either in worth or in title."

Armostes said, "Contain yourself, my lord. Ixion, aiming to embrace Juno, had sex with only a cloud, and begat Centaurs; it is a useful moral."

Ixion, a mortal, wanted to have sex with Juno, a goddess. Since she was a goddess, she was out of his league. Similarly, Calantha, a princess, was out of Ithocles' league.

Armostes continued, "Ambition hatched in clouds of pure fantasy proves in birth to be only a monster."

Ithocles said, "I thank you, yet, with your license, I should seem uncharitable to gentler fate, if, relishing the dainties of a soul's settled peace, I were so feeble that I would not digest it."

Calantha had given him a ring; this showed that she was interested in him. Ithocles would be feeble not to follow up on her interest.

Armostes said, "He deserves small trust who is not privy counselor to himself."

Nearchus, Amelus, and Orgilus entered the room.

Nearchus said about Ithocles, "Defy me!"

Orgilus said, "Your excellence mistakes his disposition, for Ithocles in the fashion of his mind is beautiful, soft, and gentle — he is the clear mirror of absolute perfection."

Amelus asked Ithocles, "Was it your modesty that called any of the prince's servants a 'spaniel'? Your nurse, surely, taught you other language than that."

Ithocles said, "Language!"

Nearchus said sarcastically, "A gallant man-at-arms is here, an expert in feats of chivalry, blunt and rough-spoken, intolerant of the bombast of civility, which less rash spirits call good manners!"

Ithocles said, "Manners!"

Orgilus said to Nearchus, "Say no more, illustrious sir; this is matchless Ithocles."

Nearchus said to Ithocles, "You might have understood who I am."

Ithocles replied, "Yes, I did; otherwise — but the presence of royalty calmed the affront. You are cousin to the princess."

Ithocles had been insulted by Amelus, but the presence of the princess had made him refrain from violence.

Nearchus said, "And I am cousin to the king, too."

Nearchus was King Amyclas' first cousin, once removed.

He continued, "A certain instrument that lent support to your colossal greatness — I am cousin to that king, too, you might have added. That king who has favored you and made you great."

The King of Sparta had added to Ithocles' greatness by rewarding him for his military valor, but Nearchus was biologically related to the king, something that he believed elevated his social position more than being victorious in battle.

Nearchus also believed that being related to the King of Sparta elevated his social position more than being related to the Princess of Sparta.

Ithocles said, "There is more divinity in beauty than in majesty."

Ithocles was elevating the beautiful Calantha above her father the king, an idea that this society would not agree with. Being more loyal to the princess than to the king was like a heresy to this society.

Armostes said, "Oh, bah, bah!"

Nearchus said, "This odd youth's pride turns heretic in loyalty. Sirrah! Low mushrooms never rival cedars."

"Sirrah" was a term used to address a man of lower status than the speaker.

The low mushroom, which grows in a night but is soft and does not last long, is analogous to an upstart. The cedar is analogous to royalty such as princes and kings.

Nearchus and Amelus exited.

Ithocles shouted, "Come back!"

He then said, more quietly, "What a pitiful dull thing am I to be tamely scolded at!"

He shouted again, "Come back!"

He then said, more quietly, "Let him come back, and echo once again that scornful sound of 'mushroom'! Painted colts — like heralds' coats gilt over with crowns and scepters — may torment a muzzled lion."

The muzzled lion was Ithocles himself, who loved Calantha but would not fight her noble relatives. The painted colt was Nearchus, a young man with high position. The herald's coat decorated with crowns and scepters was Amelus, Nearchus' friend.

Armostes said, "Nephew, nephew, your tongue is not your friend."

Orgilus said, "Concerning a point of honor, discretion knows no bounds."

Armostes was trying to calm Ithocles down; Orgilus was cunningly trying to inflame Ithocles.

Orgilus continued, "Amelus told me that it was all about a little ring."

Ithocles said, "A ring that the princess threw away, and I picked up. Admit that she threw it to me, and then what arm of brass can snatch it away from me? No; if he could grind the hoop to powder, he might sooner reach my heart than steal and wear one mote of dust of it.

"Orgilus, I am extremely wronged."

Orgilus replied, "A lady's favor is not to be so slighted."

"Slighted!" Ithocles said.

Armostes said, "Quiet these vain unruly passions, which will grow into a madness."

Orgilus said, "Griefs will have their vent."

Tecnicus entered the room; he was carrying a scroll.

"Welcome," Armostes said. "You have come at a good season, reverend man. You can pour the balm of a softening, relieving patience into the festering wound of Ithocles' ill-spent fury."

Orgilus wondered, *What is Tecnicus doing here?*

Tecnicus said, "The hurts are yet but destined to be mortal, which shortly will prove deadly. Armostes, see that you safely deliver to the king this sealed-up scroll containing counsel; bid him to peruse with fortitude the secrets of the gods."

The scroll contained Tecnicus' interpretation of the prophecy brought back from the Oracle at Delphi.

An oracle is a priest or priestess who, under the influence of a god, prophesies. The Delphic Oracle was under the influence of Apollo, god of prophecy.

Tecnicus mourned, "Oh, Sparta! Oh, Lacedaemon! Double-named, but one in fate. When kingdoms reel — pay attention to my wise saying — the heads of those kingdoms must necessarily be giddy.

"Tell the king that henceforth he no more must inquire after my aged head; Apollo wills it so. I am going to Delphi."

Armostes asked, "You aren't leaving without some conversation with our great master the king?"

Tecnicus replied, "Never more will I see him. A greater prince — the god Apollo — commands me."

He then said, "Ithocles, listen carefully."

He then recited these words from the oracle:

"*When youth is ripe, and [a person of old] age from time [life] does part,*

"*The lifeless trunk shall wed the broken heart.*"

Ithocles asked, "What does this mean, if understood correctly?

Tecnicus then said, "Listen, Orgilus. Remember what I told you long before. These tears shall be my witness."

In 1.3, Tecnicus had given advice to Orgilus.

The tears were witness that what he had said was true: It was good advice. The tears were also witness that he did not believe that Orgilus would follow that good advice.

Armostes said, "Alas, good man!"

Tecnicus then recited these words from the oracle:

"*Let craft with courtesy a while confer,*

"*Revenge proves [to be] its own executioner.*"

Orgilus said, "Dark sentences are for Apollo's priests; I am not Oedipus."

Oedipus was a solver of riddles. He had solved the riddle of the Sphinx: "What goes on four legs in the morning, two legs at noon, and three legs in the evening?"

The answer to the riddle is Man, who crawls on all fours as a baby, walks on two legs as an adult, and walks with the assistance of a cane as an old man.

Tecnicus said, "My hour of departure has come. Cheer up the king; farewell to all. Oh, Sparta! Oh, Lacedaemon!"

He exited.

Armostes said, "If prophetic fire has warmed this old man's bosom, we might construe his words to have a fatal sense."

Ithocles said, "Leave to the powers above us the effects of their decrees. My burden lies within me. Servile fears prevent no great consequences.

"Divine Calantha!"

Armostes said, "May the gods be always propitious!"

Ithocles and Armostes exited, leaving Orgilus behind.

Orgilus said to himself, "Something oddly the book-man prated, yet he spoke it while weeping:

"'Let craft with courtesy a while confer,

"'Revenge proves [to be] its own executioner.'"

A man of courtesy was Ithocles, who had reformed and now repented his previous sins against Orgilus. Orgilus, a man of crafty plotting, would confer with Ithocles.

Orgilus continued, "Consider it carefully again — for what? It shall not puzzle me. It is the dotage of a withered brain.

"Penthea did not forbid me from being in her presence, although she forbade me from appearing to her in language, message, or letter. Therefore, I may see her and gaze my fill. Why see her, then, I may, when, if I lack courage to speak — I must be silent."

Bassanes and his servants Grausis and Phulas were talking together in a room in Bassanes' house. Bassanes had repented his jealousy and his unfair treatment of his wife, Penthea.

Bassanes said to his servants, "Please, engage in your recreations; all the service I will expect is quietness among you. Take liberty at home, abroad, at all times, and in your charities appease the gods, whom I, with my distractions, have offended."

Grausis said, "I wish fair blessings on your heart!"

Phulas thought, *Here's a splendid change! My lord, to cure the itch, is surely gelded. The cuckold — that is, cuckold in his own imagination — has thrown away his horns.*

Bassanes said, "Go to your various activities, and in anything I have heretofore been faulty, let your interpretations mildly pass over my faults. Henceforth I'll study reformation; I will have no other employment."

Grausis said, "Oh, sweet man! You are truly the 'Honeycomb of Honesty.'"

Phulas said, "He is the 'Garland of Goodwill.'"

The *Honeycomb of Honesty* and the *Garland of Goodwill* were popular books of the day.

He added, "Old lady, hold up your reverend snout, and trot behind me softly, as becomes a mule of ancient carriage."

In Latin, a *mulier* is a woman.

Grausis and Phulas exited.

Bassanes said to himself, "Beasts, capable only of sense and not reason, enjoy the benefit of food and ease with thankfulness. Such silly creatures, without grudging, kick not against the portion nature has bestowed. But men are endowed with reason and the use of reason to distinguish from the chaff of abject scarcity and poor food of the impoverished the quintessence, soul, and elixir of the earth's abundance, the treasures of the sea, the air, and indeed, heaven. Yet men, who are dissatisfied with these glories of creation, are truer beasts than beasts; and of those beasts I am the worst.

"I, who was made a monarch of what a heart could wish for — a chaste wife — endeavored with what lay in me to pull down that temple that was built only for adoration, and level that temple in the dust of causeless scandal.

"But, to redeem a sacrilege so impious, my humility shall pour before the deities whom I have incensed a largess of more patience than their displeased altars can require: No tempests of commotion shall disquiet the calms of my composure."

Orgilus entered the room and said, "I have found you, you patron of more horrors than the bulk of manhood, hooped about with ribs of iron, can cram within your breast."

The word "bulk" referred to the mass of men and also to one man whose ribs hooped his body.

Orgilus continued, "Bassanes, Penthea, who was cursed by your jealousies — and more so by your dotage — is left a prey to words. She is now the subject of scandal and gossip."

Bassanes said, "Exercise your trials for addition to my penance. I am resolved. Try even harder to distress me — I deserve it."

Orgilus replied, "Don't play with misery past cure: Some angry minister of fate has deposed the empress — Penthea — of her soul, her reason, from its most proper throne, but there's a newer miracle — I, I have seen Penthea's madness, and yet I still live!"

Bassanes said, "You may delude my senses, but not my judgment, which is anchored in a firm resolution. Dalliance of mirth or wit can never unfix and unsettle it. Test me yet further."

Orgilus said, "May your destructive love for her damn all your comforts to a lasting fast from every joy of life! You barren rock, because of you we are like a ship that has been split in pieces in sight of harbor."

Ithocles entered the room along with Penthea, whose hair was let down about her ears: This was a sign of insanity. She was crying. Armostes, Philema, and Chrystalla also entered the room.

Ithocles said to Penthea, "Sister, look up. Your Ithocles, your brother, speaks to you; why do you weep? Dear, don't turn away from me —"

He added, "Here is a killing sight.

"Look, Bassanes, see a lamentable object!"

Orgilus asked Bassanes, "Man, do you see it? Sports are more gamesome and full of fun; am I yet in merriment? Why don't you laugh?"

Bassanes said to Penthea, "Divine and best of ladies, please forget my outrage; mercy cannot but lodge under a roof so excellent. I have cast off that cruelty of frenzy that once appeared to be playing an imposture on me to manipulate me into behaving badly and then played tricks on me to cheat my sleeps of rest."

Orgilus sarcastically asked Bassanes, "Was I in earnest when I told you that Penthea is insane?"

Penthea said, "Sure, if we were all Sirens, we should sing pitifully. And it would be a comely music, when while taking different parts of the song, one sings another's knell. The turtledove sighs when he has lost his mate; and yet some say he must be dead first. It is a fine deceit to pass away in a dream; indeed, I've slept with my eyes open a great while. No falsehood equals a broken faith; there's not a hair that sticks on my head but, like a leaden plummet, it sinks me to the grave. I must creep thither; the journey is not long."

Ithocles said, "But you, Penthea, have many years of life, I hope, to number yet, before you can travel that way — to the grave."

Bassanes said, "Let the sun first be wrapped up in an everlasting darkness, before the light of nature, chiefly formed for the whole world's delight, feels an eclipse so universal!"

To Bassanes, Penthea was the light of nature. To Bassanes, it was better that the sun be darkened forever than for Penthea's light to be darkened in a grave.

Orgilus said about Bassanes, "Wisdom, you see, begins to rave!"

He then said to Bassanes, "Are you insane, too, antiquity?"

Bassanes was an older man.

Penthea said, "Since I was first a wife, I might have been mother to many pretty prattling babes. They would have smiled when I smiled, and certainly I would have cried when they cried.

"Truly, brother, my father would have picked me out a husband, and then my little ones would have been no bastards. But it is too late for me to marry now; I am past childbearing. It is not my fault."

In her madness, Penthea had been starving herself; possibly, she was no longer capable of menstruating.

Bassanes said, "Fall on me, if there be a burning Aetna volcano, and bury me in flames! Sweats as hot as sulphur boil through my pores! Affliction has in store no torture as bad as seeing Penthea insane."

Orgilus said sarcastically, "Behold a patience!"

He then said to Bassanes, "Set aside your whining gray dissimulation, and do something worthy enough to be written in a chronicle of history. Show justice upon the author of this mischief; dig out the jealousies that hatched this thralldom first with your own dagger. Every antic rapture — foolish frenzy — can roar as your frenzy does."

"Show justice upon the author" meant "stab yourself and commit suicide." The author is Bassanes, but another author may also be Ithocles.

Ithocles said, "Orgilus, stop."

Bassanes said, "Don't disturb him! He is a talking puppet provided for my torment. What a fool am I to bandy passion! Before I'll speak a word, I will look on and burst."

Penthea said to Orgilus, "I loved you once."

Orgilus replied, "You did, wronged creature, in despite of malice, and because of it I love you forever."

The malice done to her was not allowing her to marry Orgilus. Additional malice done to her was Bassanes' jealousy.

Penthea said, "Give me your hand. Believe me, I'll not hurt it."

Orgilus said, "I give you my heart, too."

Penthea said, "Don't complain although I wring it hard."

She held his hand and said, "I'll kiss it. Oh, it is a fine soft palm!

"Listen, in your ear."

She whispered in his ear, "Like whom do I look, please tell me?

"No, no whispering.

"Goodness! We would have been happy; too much happiness will make folk proud, they say — but that is he" — she pointed at Ithocles — "and yet he paid for it fully. Alas, his heart has crept into the cabinet of the princess."

The word "cabinet" means 1) private chamber or 2) jewel box.

She was indirectly saying that Ithocles was in love with Calantha.

Penthea continued, "We shall have tagged laces and bride-laces."

Tagged laces are used to tie clothing, and bride-laces are used to tie sprigs of rosemary, which signifies remembrance. Both are wedding favors.

She continued, "Remember, when we last gathered roses in the garden, I found my wits, but truly you lost yours."

She hesitated, and then she pointed to Ithocles again and said, "That's he, and still it is he."

Ithocles said, "Poor soul, how deliriously her fancies guide her tongue!"

He did not want anyone to know that he was in love with Calantha.

Bassanes thought, *Keep inside me, vexation, and don't break out into a clamor. I must suppress my grief.*

Orgilus thought, *She has tutored me. Some powerful inspiration reproves my laziness.*

He believed that he needed to quickly get revenge on those who had thwarted his and Penthea's love.

He said out loud, "Now let me kiss your hand, grieved beauty."

Penthea said, "Kiss it."

He kissed her hand, and she said, "Ah, ah, his lips are wondrously cold. Dear soul, he has lost his color."

Penthea then said to Orgilus, "Have you seen a straying heart? All crannies! Every drop of blood is turned to an amethyst, which married bachelors hang in their ears."

Orgilus was the married bachelor. Penthea believed that in a way she was married to him, but he was a bachelor because they had never consummated their "marriage."

Orgilus said, "May Peace usher her into Elysium!"

He thought, *If this is madness, then madness is an oracle. In her madness, Penthea has told me to seek revenge.*

Orgilus exited.

Ithocles said, "Chrystalla, Philema, when has my sister slept? Her ravings are so wild!"

"Sir, she has not slept these past ten days," Chrystalla replied.

"We watch by her continually," Philema said. "Besides her lack of sleep, we cannot in any way persuade her to eat."

"Oh, misery of miseries!" Bassanes said.

"Take comfort," Penthea said to him. "You may live well, and die a good old man."

She then seemed to be talking to Crotolon, who was not present: "By yea and nay, an oath not to be broken, I say that if you had joined our hands once in the temple — it was since my father died, for had he lived he would have done it — I must have called you father-in-law."

She then said, "Oh, my wracked honor! Ruined by those tyrants — a cruel brother and a desperate dotage!"

The "cruel brother" was Ithocles, and the "desperate dotage" was Bassanes.

Penthea then said, "There is no peace left for a ravished wife widowed by lawless marriage; to all memory Penthea's — poor Penthea's — name is strumpeted. Everyone calls her a strumpet. But since her blood was seasoned by the forfeit of noble shame with mixtures of pollution, may her blood — it is just — be henceforth never heightened with taste of sustenance! Starve; let that fullness whose excess has fevered faith and modesty —"

She stopped and then said, "Forgive me. Oh, I faint!"

She fell into the arms of her attendants Chrystalla and Philema.

Armostes said, "Be not so willful, sweet niece, that you cause your own destruction."

Penthea could cause her own destruction by refusing to eat.

Ithocles said, "Nature will call her daughter a monster!"

All of us are sons and daughters of Nature. A law of Nature is that we eat. If Penthea refuses to eat, then she is unnatural and she is a monster.

Ithocles continued, "What! Not eat? Refuse the only ordinary means that are ordained for life? My sister, don't be a murderess to yourself."

He then asked, "Do you hear this, Bassanes? Did you hear what my sister said?"

Bassanes replied, "Bah! I am busy, for haven't I enough thoughts to think?

"All shall be well soon. It is tumbling in my head that there is an expert skill that will fatten and keep smooth the outside of a person, yes, and comfort the vital spirits without the help of food. Fumes or perfumes will do it. Perfumes or fumes. Let her alone; I'll search out the trick of it."

In this society, some people believed that nourishment could be gotten from odors.

Penthea said, "Lead me gently; may the heavens reward you. Griefs are sure friends; they leave, without control, neither cure nor comforts for a leprous soul."

The "leprous soul" belonged to Penthea.

Chrystalla and Philema helped Penthea to exit.

Bassanes said, "I grant to you and will put in practice immediately what you shall always wonder at and admire. It is wonderful; it is super-singular and not to be matched. Yet, when I've done it, I've done it— you shall all thank me."

He exited.

Armostes said, "This sight is full of terror."

Ithocles said, "On my soul lies such an infinite impediment of massive dullness that I have not sense enough to feel it."

Nearchus and Amelus entered the room.

"See, uncle," Ithocles said, "the angry thing returns again. Shall we welcome him with thunder? We are haunted, and we must use exorcism to conjure down this spirit of malevolence."

"Mildly, nephew," Armostes said.

Nearchus said politely to Ithocles, "I come not, sir, to chide your late unmannerly conduct because I am sure that there is an inurement to a roughness in soldiers of your years and fortunes, chiefly, so recently prosperous, and that you have not yet shaken off the custom of the war in hours of leisure. As a military man, you are not accustomed to use courtly manners.

"Nor shall you need to excuse your conduct to me, since you are to render that account to that fair excellence, the Princess Calantha, who in her private gallery awaits you and expects to hear it from your own mouth alone.

"I am a messenger but only for her pleasure."

Ithocles bowed and said, "Excellent Nearchus, be prince always of my services, and conquer without the combat of dispute. I honor you."

Nearchus then said, "King Amyclas is suddenly indisposed. Physicians have been called for. It is fitting, Armostes, that you should be near him."

Armostes said, "Sir, I kiss your hands."

Ithocles and Armostes exited.

Nearchus said to his friend, "Amelus, I perceive that Calantha's bosom is warmed with fires other than such as can take strength from any fuel of the love I might address to her. Young Ithocles, unless I am mistaken, is the lord ascendant of her devotions; he is one, to speak about him truly, who is in every disposition nobly fashioned. Calantha loves Ithocles, not me."

Amelus asked, "But can your highness brook to be so rivaled, considering the inequality of the persons?"

Nearchus and Calantha were both of a higher social class than Ithocles.

Nearchus replied, "I can, Amelus; for affections injured by tyranny or rigor of compulsion, like tempest-threatened trees that are not firmly rooted, never spring to timely growth. Observe, for instance, life-spent Penthea and unhappy Orgilus."

Amelus asked, "What does your grace intend to do?"

Nearchus replied, "To be jealous in public of what privately I'll further, and although they shall not know it, yet they shall find it."

In public, he would pretend to be jealous, but in private, without their knowing it, he would advance the courtship of Ithocles and Calantha.

Hemophil and Groneas helped King Amyclas sit on a chair in a room in the palace. Armostes, carrying a box, entered the room. With him were Crotolon and Prophilus.

"Our daughter is not near?" King Amyclas asked.

"She has retired, sir," Armostes said, "into her gallery."

"Where is Nearchus, the prince our cousin?" King Amyclas asked.

"He just now walked into the grove, my lord," Prophilus answered.

Using the royal plural, King Amyclas ordered, "Everyone leave us except Armostes and you, Crotolon. We want some privacy."

Prophilus said, "Health unto your majesty!"

Prophilus, Hemophil, and Groneas exited.

"What!" King Amyclas said. "Tecnicus is gone?"

"He has gone to Delphi," Armostes said, "and to your royal hands he presents this box."

"Unseal it, good Armostes," King Amyclas said. "Therein lie the secrets of the oracle; take the scroll out."

Armostes took out the scroll.

"May Apollo live as our patron!" King Amyclas said. "Read the scroll, Armostes."

Armostes read the scroll out loud:

"The plot in which the vine takes root

"Begins to dry from head to foot;

"The stock soon withering, want [lack] of sap

"Does cause to quail [wither away] the budding grape;

"But from the neighboring elm a dew

"Shall drop, and feed the plot anew. "

"That is the oracle," King Amyclas said. "What interpretation does the philosopher Tecnicus make?"

Armostes replied, "This brief one only."

He read out loud the interpretation:

"The plot is Sparta, the dried vine the king;

"The quailing [withering-away] grape his daughter; but the thing

"Of most importance, not to be revealed
"Is a near prince, the elm: the rest [is] concealed.
"Tecnicus. "

"Enough," King Amyclas said. "Although the expounding of this riddle is itself a riddle, yet we construe how near our laboring age draws to a rest. The oracle says that I will die.

"But must Calantha quail, wither, and fail, too? That young grape untimely budded! I could mourn for her. Her tenderness has of yet deserved no rigor to be so crossed by fate."

Armostes said, "You misapply, sir — with your permission let me speak — what Apollo, god of prophecy, has clouded in hidden sense. I here conjecture Calantha's marriage with some neighboring prince, the dew of which befriending elm shall ever strengthen your subjects with a sovereignty of power."

Crotolon said, "Besides, most gracious lord, the pith of oracles is to be digested when the outcomes expound their truth, not brought to light as soon as uttered. Truth is the child of Time; and here in this oracle I find no troubling point; rather, I find a cause of comfort with the unity of kingdoms."

Amyclas said, "May it prove to be so, for the good and the well-being of this dear nation!"

He then asked, "Where is Ithocles?"

He added, "Armostes, Crotolon, when this withered vine of my frail carcass is fired on the funeral pile into its ashes, let that young man be hedged about always with your cares and loves. Much I owe to his worth; much I owe to his service."

He then said, "Let the people waiting outside come in now."

Armostes ordered, "All attend here!"

Calantha, Ithocles, Prophilus, Orgilus, Euphrania, Hemophil, and Groneas all entered the room.

"Dear sir!" Calantha said. "King! Father!"

"Oh, my royal master!" Ithocles said.

King Amyclas said, "Cleave not my heart, sweet twins of my life's solace, with your forejudging fears; there is no medicine so cunningly restorative to cheer and treat with care the fall of age, or call back youth and vigor, as your consents in duty. I will shake off this languishing disease of time, to quicken fresh pleasures in these drooping hours of sadness.

"Is fair Euphrania married yet to Prophilus?"

Crotolon replied, "They were married this morning, gracious lord."

"This very morning," Orgilus said, "which, with your highness' permission, you may observe, too. Our sister looks, I think, mirthful and sprightly, as if her chaster fancy could already expound the riddle of her gain in losing a trifle maidens know only that they know not."

He was referring to his sister's losing her virginity. Maidens — that is, virgins — know only that they don't know what sex is like. Once married, they lose their maidenhood and lack of knowledge of sex.

Euphrania, his sister, blushed.

"Pish!" Orgilus said. "Please, don't blush. It is only an honest change of fashion in the garment, loose for strait, and so the modest maiden is made a wife."

Wives become pregnant, and then they exchange their clothing that is tight in the waist for clothing that is loose in the waist.

Orgilus was also punning bawdily. Straight-laced maidens marry and then become, in a way, loose women when their laces are loosened for sex.

He added, "Shrewd business — isn't it, sister?"

The word "shrewd" can mean 1) wicked and 2) painful.

"You are pleasant," Euphrania said. "You are making jokes."

"We thank you, Orgilus," King Amyclas said. "This mirth becomes you.

"But why does the court sit in such a silence? A wedding without revels is not seemly."

Calantha replied, "Your recent indisposition, sir, forbade revelry."

King Amyclas said, "Let it be your charge, Calantha, to set forward the bridal sports, to which I will be present. If I can't be present, I'll be at least consenting.

"My own Ithocles, I have done little for you yet."

Ithocles replied, "You have built me to the full height I stand in."

Calantha thought, *It's now or never!*

She then said to her father, "May I propose a suit? May I ask you for something?"

King Amyclas replied, "Request it, and you shall have it."

Calantha said, "Please, sir, give me this young man, and no further account him yours than he deserves in all things to be thought worth mine. I will esteem him according to his merit."

Of course, both King Amyclas and Calantha believed that Ithocles had high merit.

King Amyclas said to Calantha, "Always you are my daughter; always you grow upon my heart."

He said to Ithocles, "Give me your hand."

He then joined the hands of Ithocles and Calantha and said, "Calantha, take your own. In noble actions you'll find him firm and absolute."

He added, "I would not have parted with you, Ithocles, to anyone except to a mistress who is all what I am."

Ithocles said, "That is a change, great king, most wished for, because the change is for the same."

Calantha whispered to Ithocles, "You are mine. Have I now kept my word?"

Ithocles whispered to Calantha, "Divinely."

Earlier, Nearchus had told Ithocles to go and see Calantha at her request. The two had met and confessed their love for each other, and Calantha had promised to persuade her father the king to allow them to marry, something he had just now agreed to do.

The conversation among King Amyclas, Calantha, and Ithocles had been quiet. Only Orgilus had overheard.

Orgilus thought about Ithocles, *Rich fortune's guard — the favor of a princess — rock you, brave man, in ever-crowned plenty! You are the darling of the time; be thankful for it. Ho! Here's a swing in destiny — apparently! Ithocles the youth is up on tiptoe, yet he may stumble.*

King Amyclas said, "Go to your recreations and entertainments."

He ordered some servants, "Now convey me to my bed-chamber."

He then said, "Let no one wear a distempered look on his forehead."

All replied, "May the gods preserve you!"

Calantha whispered to Ithocles, "Sweetheart, don't be out of my sight."

Ithocles whispered to Calantha, "You are my entire happiness!"

Everyone exited, with some servants carrying the king.

Orgilus stopped Ithocles, making him be out of Calantha's sight.

"Shall I be bold, my lord?" Orgilus asked. "Shall I be presumptuous?"

Ithocles said, "You cannot be presumptuous to me, Orgilus, because you are my friend. Call me your own, for Prophilus must henceforth be all your sister's. Friendship, although it doesn't cease with a marriage, yet is often at less command than when a single freedom can dispose it. Friendship can continue after one friend marries, but less time is available to enjoy it."

Orgilus said, "That is very right, my most good lord, my most great lord, my gracious princely lord, and I might add, royal."

Ithocles did not know that Orgilus had overheard King Amyclas approving the marriage of Calantha and him, and so he pretended to be surprised: "Royal! Can a subject be royal?"

"Why not, please, sir?" Orgilus replied. "The sovereignty of kingdoms in their early stages stooped to merit, not birth; there's as much merit in clearness of affection, aka the purity of love, as in puddle of generation, aka the murkiness and uncertainty of heredity. You have conquered love even in the loveliest; if I err not greatly, the son of Venus has bequeathed to the control of you, Ithocles, his quiver by whose arrows Calantha's breast is opened."

"Can it be possible?" Ithocles asked.

"I was myself a bit of a suitor once and forward in preferment, too," Orgilus said. "I was so forward that, speaking truly, I may without offence, sir, presume to whisper that my hopes, and — listen carefully — my certainty of marriage stood assured with as firm footing — by your leave — as any is now at this very instant, but —"

"It is granted," Ithocles interrupted. "And for a league of privacy between you and me, read over my bosom and learn a secret: The princess is contracted to be my wife."

Orgilus said, "Yes, and why not? I now applaud her wisdom. I dare pronounce that you will be a just monarch when your kingdom stands seated in your will, secure and settled. Greece must wonder and tremble at you."

Ithocles and Orgilus began to mention good and "good" things that would follow when Ithocles became the husband of Calantha and the King of Sparta.

Ithocles said, "Then the sweetness of so imparadised a comfort, Orgilus! It is to banquet with the gods."

Orgilus said, "The glory of numerous children, potency of nobles, bent knees, hearts paved to tread on!"

Orgilus' heart had been trodden on.

Ithocles said, "With a friendship so dear, so fast as yours is."

Orgilus said, "I am unfit for office; but for service —"

Ithocles interrupted, "We'll distinguish our fortunes merely in the title; partners in all respects except the bed."

Orgilus said, "The bed! Forbid it Jove's own jealousy! Until finally we slip down in the common earth together, and there our beds are equal, except for some monument to show this was the king, and this was the subject."

Soft, sad music played on a lute.

"Listen, what sad sounds are these?" Orgilus asked. "They are extremely sad ones."

Ithocles said, "Surely, they come from Penthea's lodgings."

Orgilus said, "Listen! There is a voice, too."

Philema sang this song while Chrystalla played the lute:

"Oh, no more, no more, too late

"Sighs are spent; the burning tapers

"Of a life as chaste as fate,

"Pure as are unwritten papers,

"Are burnt out: No heat, no light

"Now remains; it is ever [always] night.

"Love is dead; let lovers' eyes,

"Locked in endless dreams,

"The extremes of all extremes,

"Ope [Open] no more, for now Love dies,

"Now Love dies — implying

"Love's martyrs must be ever, ever dying. "

"Oh, my misgiving heart!" Ithocles said.

"A horrid stillness succeeds this deathful air," Orgilus said. "Let's know the reason. Walk quietly. There is mystery in mourning."

Penthea was dead. In her apartment in the palace, her body reclined on a chair. She was veiled. With her were Chrystalla and Philema, sitting at her feet and mourning.

Two other servants brought in two chairs, one on Penthea's right side and one on her left. Orgilus had specially ordered a modification to one of the chairs.

As the servants left the apartment, Ithocles and Orgilus arrived.

A servant whispered to Orgilus, "It is done; the trick chair is on her right side."

"Good," Orgilus whispered back. "Leave now."

The two servants exited.

Ithocles said, "May soft peace enrich this room!"

Orgilus asked, "How fares the lady?"

"Dead!" Philema said.

"Dead!" Chrystalla said.

"Starved!" Philema said.

"Starved! " Chrystalla said.

Ithocles said, "Wretched me!"

Orgilus requested, "Tell us how she departed from her life."

Philema replied, "She called for music, and begged some gentle voice to sing a farewell to life and griefs. Chrystalla touched the lute; I wept the funeral song."

Chrystalla said, "The funeral song was scarcely ended when her last breath sealed up these hollow sounds: 'Oh, cruel Ithocles and injured Orgilus!' So down she drew her veil, and so died."

Ithocles said, "So died!"

Orgilus said to Chrystalla and Philema, who were sitting at Penthea's feet, "Get up! You are messengers of death; go away from us. Here's woe enough to court without a prompter. Go away, and — listen carefully — until you see us again, say no syllable about her being dead. Leave, keep a smooth brow, and don't reveal that you are grieving."

Chrystalla and Philema exited.

Orgilus began, "My lord —"

Ithocles interrupted, "My only sister! Another is not left me."

"Take that chair," Orgilus said, motioning to the chair on Penthea's right. "I'll seat myself here in this chair. Between us sits the object of our sorrows; some few tears we'll part among us. I perhaps can put together one lamentable story to prepare our eyes to cry. There, there; sit there, my lord."

Ithocles said, "Yes, as you please."

Ithocles sat down, and his arms were caught and restrained by the trick chair.

He asked, "What is the meaning of this treachery?"

"Caught!" Orgilus said. "You are caught, young master; it is your throne of coronation, you fool of greatness!"

He went over to Penthea and removed her veil, saying, "See, I take this veil off. Survey a beauty withered by the flames of an insulting, arrogant Phaëton, her brother."

Ithocles asked, "Do you mean to kill me basely?"

To kill him while he had no chance to defend himself would be to kill him basely.

Orgilus replied, "I foreknew the last act of her life, and I lured you here in order to sacrifice a tyrant to a turtledove."

He now began to accuse Ithocles of being motivated by political ambition and the ambition of enjoying the good things of life. To Orgilus, that would account for Ithocles' giving Penthea in marriage to Bassanes and for his courtship of Calantha.

Orgilus continued, "You dreamed of kingdoms, did you? You dreamed of how to take to your bosom the delicacies of a young princess. You dreamed of how with this nod to show grace to that subtle courtier. You dreamed of how with that frown to make this noble tremble, and so forth.

"Meanwhile, Penthea's groans and tortures, her agonies, her miseries, and her afflictions, never touched upon your thought. As for my injuries, alas, they were beneath your royal pity. But yet they lived, you proud man, to destroy you.

"Behold your fate — this steel!"

Orgilus drew a dagger.

"Strike your dagger home in my heart!" Ithocles said. "My courage, which is as keen as your revenge, shall give it welcome. But please don't faint; if the wound closes up, probe it with double force, and search it deeply. You think that I will whine and beg for compassion. You think that I will be loath to leave the vainness of my glories.

"A statelier resolution arms my confidence: I want to cheat you of honor. Nor could I engage in an equal trial of unequal fortune by hazard of a duel; it would be a bravery too mighty for a slave intending murder."

Ithocles was not willing to engage Orgilus in a duel. Ithocles was higher born than Orgilus, and he believed that he would degrade himself if he fought a duel with a person of Orgilus' social rank.

He continued, "Go on to the execution, and inherit a conflict with your horrors."

The conflict could be mental: Orgilus could come to feel guilt as a result of this murder. Or Ithocles may have meant that his murder would be avenged.

Orgilus said, "By Apollo, you talk splendid talk! For requital I will talk about you to your mistress richly and I will take this peaceful thought along with me: After a few short minutes have elapsed, my resolves shall quickly follow your wrathful ghost."

Orgilus intended to die soon.

He continued, "Then, if we compete for mastery in the afterlife, Penthea's sacred eyes shall lend me new courage.

"Give me your hand. Be healthful in your parting from lost mortality! Thus, thus I free it."

He held one of Ithocles' hands as he stabbed Ithocles, giving him a mortal wound.

Ithocles said, "Still, still, I scorn to shrink in fear."

Orgilus said, "Keep up your spirit: I will be gentle even in shedding blood; to prolong pain, which I strive to cure, would be cruel."

He stabbed Ithocles again.

Ithocles said, "You who are nimble in vengeance, I forgive you. May spiritual safety follow my forgiveness, with best success: Oh, may it prosper!

"Penthea, by your side your brother bleeds. This is the payment of his wrongs to your forced faith: I made you marry a man whom you did not want to marry.

"Thoughts of ambition, or delicious banquet with beauty, youth, and love, together perish in my last breath, which on the sacred altar of a long-looked-for peace now moves to heaven."

He died.

Orgilus said, "Farewell, fair spring of manhood! Henceforth welcome the best expectation of a noble sufferance.

"I'll lock the bodies somewhere safe, until what must follow shall happen."

He then said about the twins Penthea and Ithocles: "Sweet twins, shine as stars forever!"

He added, "In vain they build their hopes whose life is shame. No monument lasts except a happy name."

CHAPTER 5

— 5.1 —

Bassanes stood alone in a room in his house.

He said to himself, "Athens — to Athens I have sent, the nursery of Greece for learning and the fountain of knowledge; for here in Sparta there's not left among us one wise man to direct; we're all turned madcaps.

"It is said that Apollo is the god of herbs, and so then certainly he knows the virtue of them: To Delphos I have sent, too. If there can be a help for nature, we are sure yet."

Because he did not yet know that Penthea was dead, he was still trying to find a cure for her.

Orgilus entered the room and said, "May honor attend your counsels forever!"

Bassanes replied, "I ask you with all my heart to let me go away from you quietly. I will not have anything to do with you, of all men.

"The doubles of a hare, or in a morning greetings from a splay-footed witch; to drop three drops of blood at the nose, just three and no more; the croaking of ravens, or the screech of owls are not as boding evils as your crossing my private meditations."

All the things he had mentioned were bad omens. The doubles of a hare are the hunted hare's quick turns made while fleeing a predator. A hare's crossing a highway in front of one was regarded as a bad omen, especially for older people such as Bassanes.

Bassanes continued, "Shun me, please. And if I cannot love you heartily, I'll love you as well as I can."

"Noble Bassanes," Orgilus said, "don't mistake me."

Bassanes said, "Bah! Then we — Penthea and I — shall be troubled. You were ordained to be my plague — may heaven make me thankful, and may heaven give me patience, too, heaven, I ask you."

Orgilus said, "Accept a league of amity and friendship; for henceforth, I vow, by my best guardian spirit, in a syllable, never to speak words of vexation to you. I will pursue service and friendship to you with a zealous sorrow for my past incivility towards you."

Bassanes said, "Heyday, these are good words, good words! I must believe them, and be a coxcomb — fool — for my labor."

Orgilus said, "Don't use so hard a language; your mistrust of me has no cause. For example, if you promise to put on a constancy of patience, such a patience as chronicle or history has never mentioned, as follows no precedent, but shall stand as a wonder and a theme for imitation — your example will be the first, pointing to a second — I will acquaint you with an unmatched secret, whose knowledge shall set an end to your griefs."

The unmatched secret was the deaths of Penthea and Ithocles.

Bassanes said, "You cannot set an end to my griefs, Orgilus. That is in the power of the gods only. Yet for satisfaction, because I note a seriousness in your utterance, unforced and naturally free, be assured that the virgin-bays shall not stand against the lightning with more contempt of danger than my steadfastness shall withstand the full content of your unmatched secret."

A superstition of the time stated that lightning would not strike bay trees, aka laurel trees.

He continued, "Even if your unmatched secret could make a senseless marble statue distracted and perturbed, it would find that I am a rock.

"I expect now to hear some truth of unprecedented importance."

Orgilus said, "To your patience you must add privacy, as strong in silence as the mysteries locked up in Jove's own bosom. You must not tell others what I tell you."

Bassanes said, "A skull hid in the earth for a treble age shall sooner prate your secret than I shall."

Orgilus said, "Lastly, you ought to give your obedience to such direction as the severity of a glorious action deserves to lead your wisdom and your judgment."

Bassanes replied, "I will, with the assurance of my will and thankfulness."

Orgilus added, "And with manly courage. Please, then, follow me."

Bassanes said, "Wherever you lead me, I will not fear."

Bassanes followed Orgilus.

Many people walked into a stateroom in the palace to celebrate the wedding of Euphrania and Prophilus. Two men escorted Euphrania, the bride: Groneas and Hemophil. Two women escorted Prophilus, the groom: Chrystalla and Philema. Nearchus escorted Calantha. Crotolon and Amelus also walked into the stateroom, as did many attendants.

Calantha said, "We miss our servant Ithocles and Orgilus."

Ithocles was her servant in the sense that he loved and served her.

She then asked, "On whom do they attend? Where are they?"

Orgilus' father, Crotolon, replied, "Gracious princess, my son, whispered to me about some new dramatic performance that would be part of these revels. I conceive that Lord Ithocles and my son will be actors in that dramatic performance."

Calantha said, "That is a good excuse for their absence. As for Bassanes, delights are troublesome to him. Is Armostes with the king?"

"He is," Crotolon replied.

Calantha said, "On to the dance!

"Dear cousin Nearchus, you dance with the bride; the bridegroom must be entrusted to my courtship and dance with me.

"Don't be jealous, Euphrania; I shall scarcely prove to be a temptress to the groom.

"Let's fall to our dance."

Music played, and Nearchus danced with Euphrania, Prophilus danced with Calantha, Chrystalla danced with Hemophil, and Philema danced with Groneas.

They danced the first part of the dance, during which Armostes entered.

Armostes went to Calantha and whispered in her ear, "The king your father is dead."

Calantha said, "Let's dance the next part."

As they danced the next part, a shocked Armostes said to himself, "Is this possible?"

Bassanes entered the room and whispered to Calantha, "Oh, madam! Penthea, poor Penthea's starved to death."

Calantha said, "Curse you!"

She then said to her partner, "Lead to the next part of the dance."

Shocked, Bassanes said, "Amazement dulls my senses."

The dancers danced.

Orgilus entered the room and whispered to Calantha, "Brave Ithocles has been murdered, murdered cruelly."

Calantha said, "How dull this music sounds! Strike up the music more sprightly. Our footings are not active like our heart, which treads the nimbler measure."

Shocked, Orgilus said, "I am thunderstruck."

They danced the last part of the dance and then the music and dance stopped.

"So!" Calantha said. "Let us rest and catch our breath for a while."

She asked the ladies, "Hasn't this dance raised fresher color on your cheeks?"

Nearchus said, "Sweet princess, a perfect purity of blood enamels the beauty of your white cheeks."

Calantha said, "We all look cheerfully, and, cousin Nearchus, it is, I think, an extraordinary presumption in any who sets first our lawful pleasures before their own sour censure to bluntly interrupt the custom of this ceremony."

This was a self-criticism: Calantha was setting — or seemed to be setting — first enjoying her lawful pleasures before hearing the bad news that others were bringing to her.

Historically, the Spartans were known for their fortitude in facing grief and hardship. The Spartans respected such things as bravery in battle. A Spartan mother once told her son who was going into battle, "Either come back with your shield or on it." If her son came back without his shield, that would be evidence that he had dropped his shield in order to flee from the enemy and save his life. It would be better for him to stay and fight, even if it meant that he died in battle and his corpse had to be carried home on his shield. This type of attitude was historically admired in Sparta.

Nearchus replied, "No one dares to do that, lady."

Calantha said, "Yes, yes, they do; some hollow voice delivered to me the news that the king my father is dead."

"The king is dead," Armostes said. "That fatal news was mine; for in my arms he breathed his last, and along with his crown he bequeathed to you your mother's wedding ring, which here I give to you."

He gave her the ring.

Crotolon said, "This is very strange!"

Calantha said, "May peace crown his ashes!"

Using the royal plural, she said, "We are queen, then."

"Long live Calantha!" Nearchus shouted. "Sparta's sovereign queen!"

All shouted, "Long live the queen!"

Calantha asked, "What did Bassanes whisper?"

Bassanes replied, "That my Penthea, miserable soul, has starved to death."

"She's happy," Calantha said. "She has finished a long and painful progress."

She added, "A third murmur pierced my unwilling ears."

Orgilus said, "I whispered that Ithocles has been murdered — or rather butchered, had not the bravery of his undaunted spirit, conquering terror, proclaimed his last act to be a triumph over ruin."

"What!" Armostes said. "Murdered!"

"By whose hand?" Calantha asked.

"By my hand," Orgilus said.

He drew his dagger and said, "This weapon was the instrument of my revenge. The reasons for my murdering Ithocles are just, and known; if you were to acquit him of these reasons, then there has never lived a gentleman of greater merit, hope, or qualifications to steer a kingdom."

Crotolon said, "For shame, Orgilus!"

Euphrania said, "For shame, brother!"

Calantha asked, "You have really done it?"

Bassanes said, "Let Orgilus report how it was done, the forfeit of whose allegiance to our laws covets rigorous justice; but that the murder has been done, my eyes have seen such evidence of credit that is too sure to be confuted.

"Armostes, rend not your arteries with hearing the bare circumstances and details of these calamities."

A Spartan form of suicide was cutting arteries and bleeding to death.

Bassanes continued, "You have lost a nephew and a niece, and I have lost a wife. Continue to be a man still. Make me the pattern of enduring evils: I am a man who can outlive my mighty evils that afflict me, not shrinking at such a pressure as would sink a soul into what is most of death, the worst of horrors.

"But I have sealed a covenant with sadness, and entered into bonds without condition, to withstand these tempests calmly. I have made this agreement with Orgilus that I would not grieve. Look carefully at me, nobles. I do not shed a tear — not even for Penthea!

"This is excellent misery!"

Calantha said, "We begin our reign with a first act of justice. Unhappy Orgilus, your confession dooms you to a death sentence. But still your father's and your sister's presence shall be excused from watching you die.

"Crotolon, give a blessing to your lost son.

"Euphrania, take your farewell.

"And then both of you leave."

Crotolon said to his son, Orgilus, "Confirm yourself, you noble sorrow, in worthy resolution! The best thing you can do now is to die well."

Euphrania said, "If my tears could speak, my griefs would be slight. My grief is too great for tears."

Orgilus said, "May all goodness dwell among you!

"Enjoy my sister, Prophilus. My vengeance has never aimed at your harm."

Calantha ordered, "Now leave."

Crotolon, Prophilus, and Euphrania exited.

Calantha said to Orgilus, "Bloody relater of your stains in blood, because you have spoken with honorable mention about Ithocles, whose fortunes and life by you have both been at once snatched from him, make your choice of what death pleases you best; there's all our bounty you will get from us."

She then said to Nearchus, "But to prevent delays, let me, dear cousin, entreat you and these lords to see Orgilus' execution performed immediately — before you leave this room."

"Your will commands us," Nearchus said.

Orgilus said, "I ask one suit, just queen, my last. Give me your clemency so that no common hand divides me from this my humble frailty: my life. Let no common person perform my execution."

Calantha replied, "To their wisdoms of those who are to be spectators of your end, I refer your request. Those who are dead, are dead; had they not now died, of necessity they must have paid the debt they owed to nature at one time or another.

"Use dispatch, my lords; perform this execution quickly."

Using the royal plural, she said, "We'll immediately prepare our coronation."

Calantha, Philema, and Chrystalla exited.

Armostes said, "It is strange that these tragedies should never touch on her female pity."

Bassanes said, "She has a masculine spirit; and why then should I whine, and, like a girl, put a finger in the eye and shed tears? Let's be all toughness, without distinction between sex and sex."

Nearchus asked, "Now, Orgilus, what is your choice? How do you choose to die?"

Orgilus replied, "To bleed to death."

Armostes asked, "Who will be the executioner?"

Orgilus replied, "Myself, no surgeon. I am well skilled in letting blood."

He had experience: He had shed the blood of Ithocles.

Orgilus continued, "Bind fast this arm so that the veins may from their arteries convey a full stream of blood."

His arms would each have a strip of cloth tied around them to make the veins swell with blood.

Orgilus drew his dagger and said, "Here's a skillful instrument."

He added, "Only I am a beggar to some charity to speed me in this execution by lending the other prick to the other arm, when this arm is bubbling life out."

Orgilus would use the dagger to cut one arm, but he needed someone else to cut his other arm.

Bassanes said, "I will do it. It most concerns my art, my care, my credit."

He ordered, "Quick, tie strips of cloth around both of his arms."

Orgilus said, "Gramercy, friendship! I give great thanks to you. Such courtesies are real that flow cheerfully without an expectation of requital.

"Give me a staff in this hand."

They gave him a staff to hold and squeeze to make his veins swell with blood.

He continued, "If a proneness or custom in my nature from my cradle had been inclined to fierce and eager bloodshed, a coward guilt, hid in a coward quaking, would have betrayed my fame and reputation to ignoble flight and worthless pursuit of full-of-fear safety.

"But look upon my steadiness, and scorn not the sickness of my fortune, which, since Bassanes became husband to Penthea, had lain bedridden.

"We trifle away and waste time with words.

"Thus I show skill in opening of a vein too full, too lively."

He cut his arm with a dagger and began to bleed.

Armostes said, "Desperate courage!"

Nearchus said, "Honorable infamy!"

Hemophil said, "I tremble at the sight."

Groneas said, "I wish I were free to leave!"

Bassanes said, "His blood sparkles like a lusty wine newly tapped from a wine barrel. The vessel must be sound from which it issues."

He said to Orgilus, "Grasp hard this other stick — I'll be as nimble — but please, don't look pale — let's do it! Stretch out your arm with vigor and with unshaken virtue."

He cut Orgilus' other arm and said, "Good! Oh, I don't envy a rival suited to conquer in extremities. This pastime appears majestic; some high-tuned poem hereafter shall deliver to posterity the writer's glory and his subject's triumph — the triumph of Orgilus.

"How are you, man? Don't droop yet."

Orgilus said, "I feel no tremors.

"On a pair-royal do I wait in death. I will wait on my sovereign Amyclas, as his liegeman; on my mistress Penthea, as a devoted servant; and on Ithocles, as if no splendid, yet no unworthy enemy."

A pair-royal is a three-of-a-kind in card games.

He continued, "Nor did I use a trick chair to entrap his life out of a slavish fear to combat youth, strength, or skill, but because I dared not stake the goodness of a cause on fortune, by which his name might have outfaced my vengeance.

"Oh, Tecnicus, inspired with Phoebus' fire! I remember your augury; it was perfect:

"'*Revenge proves [to be] its own executioner.*'

"When feeble man is bending to his mother the earth, the dust he was first framed of, thus he totters."

Orgilus was feeling weak from loss of blood: He could barely stand.

Bassanes said, "Life's fountain is dried up."

Orgilus said, "So falls the ensign of my natural privilege in being a creature of earth! A mist hangs over my eyes; the sun's bright splendor is clouded in an everlasting shadow. Welcome, you ice that sits about my heart. No heat can ever thaw you."

He fell and died.

Nearchus said, "Speech has left him."

Bassanes said, "He has shaken hands with time; I will take care of his funeral urn."

He ordered some attendants, "Remove the bloodless body."

He then said, "The coronation must require attendance. That done, my few remaining days can be spent only in mourning."

— 5.3 —

In a temple stood an altar covered with white; on it were two candles of purified wax. The music of recorders sounded.

Four people carried in Ithocles on a hearse. He was wearing a rich robe and had a crown on his head. They placed him on one side of the altar. Calantha, wearing a white robe and a crown, entered the temple. Euphrania, Philema, and Chrystalla, wearing white, then entered the temple. Armostes, Crotolon, Prophilus, Amelus, Bassanes, Hemophil, and Groneas followed them.

Calantha knelt before the altar. The rest stood to the side. The women knelt, and the recorders ceased their music as Calantha prayed. Once her prayer was finished, Calantha and the rest rose, doing obeisance to the altar.

Using the royal plural, Calantha said, "Our prayers are heard; the gods are merciful.

"Now tell me, you whose loyalties pay tribute to us your lawful sovereign, how unwise your duties or obedience is to render subjection to the scepter of a virgin, you who have been ever fortunate in princes of masculine and stirring composition.

"A woman has enough work to govern wisely her own demeanors, passions, and inner discords of mind.

"A nation warlike and inured to the practice of political cunning and labor cannot endure a feminine authority. We therefore command your counsel: Advise us in the choosing of a husband whose abilities can better guide this kingdom."

"Royal lady," Nearchus said. "Your law is in your will."

Armostes said, "We have seen tokens of your constancy too recently to mistrust it. The evidence we have seen tells us that you will be a good ruler."

Crotolon said, "Yet, if your highness will settle on a choice that by your own judgment you both allow and like, Sparta may grow in power, and proceed to an increasing height."

Calantha asked Bassanes, "Are you of the same opinion?"

Bassanes replied, "Alas, great mistress, my reason is so clouded with the thick darkness of my infinite woes that I do not forecast dangers, hopes, or safety.

"Give me some corner of the world to wear out the remnant of the minutes I must number in this life. Give me some corner of the world where I may hear no sounds but the sad lamentations of virgins who have lost partners they were contracted to marry, the sad lamentations of husbands howling that their wives were raped by some untimely fate, the sad lamentations of friends divided by churlish opposition, or the sad lamentations of fathers weeping upon their children's slaughtered carcasses, or the sad lamentations of daughters groaning over their fathers' hearses, and I can dwell there, and with these keep fellowship and make as sad lamentations as theirs. We can make a concert of groans.

"What can you look for from an old, foolish, peevish, doting man but the craziness of age?"

Calantha began, "Cousin of Argos —"

Nearchus immediately asked, "Madam?"

Calantha said, "Suppose I were to immediately choose you for my lord and husband. I'll open freely what articles I would propose to treat on before our marriage."

"Name them, virtuous lady," Nearchus replied.

Calantha said, "I would presume that you would retain the royalty and sovereign power of Sparta in her own territory; that is, you would stay in Sparta and be king here.

"Then Armostes might be viceroy in Argos, Crotolon might bear sway in Messene, and Bassanes —"

Bassanes interrupted, "I, queen! Alas, what about me?"

Calantha replied, "You might be Sparta's marshal. The multitudes of high employments could not but set a peace to private griefs. If you keep busy doing important work, you will find peace.

"These gentlemen, Groneas and Hemophil, with worthy pensions, would wait upon your person in your chamber. They will be your personal attendants."

She then said, "I would bestow Chrystalla as a wife on Amelus. She'll prove to be a constant wife, and Philema would go into Vesta's Temple and be a vestal virgin."

Bassanes said, "This is a testament! This doesn't sound like conditions for a marriage!"

"All this will be performed," Nearchus said.

Calantha said, "Lastly, for Prophilus, he should be, cousin, solemnly invested with all those honors, titles, and preferments that his dear friend and my neglected husband for too short a time enjoyed."

Prophilus said, "I am unworthy to live in your remembrance."

Euphrania said, "Excellent lady!"

Nearchus asked, "Madam, what do you mean by that phrase 'neglected husband'?"

The neglected husband, of course, was Ithocles. Other than Calantha, no one still alive knew that she and Ithocles had been betrothed.

Calantha said to Nearchus, "Forgive me."

She then said, "Now I turn to you, you shadow of my contracted lord! Bear witness all as I put my mother's wedding ring upon his finger; it was my father's last bequest."

She placed the wedding ring on Ithocles' finger.

She then said, "Thus I newly marry him whose wife I am; death shall not separate us.

"Oh, my lords, I simply deceived your eyes with a grotesque performance, when one piece of news after another immediately came to inform me of death! And death! And death!

"Always I continued to dance, but the news struck home, here in my heart, and in an instant.

"There exist such mere women, who with shrieks and outcries can vow an immediate end to all their sorrows, yet they live to court new pleasures, and outlive them.

"It is the silent griefs that cut the heartstrings and break the heart.

"Let me die smiling."

Nearchus said, "This is a truth too ominous."

Calantha said, "One kiss on these cold lips, my last!"

She kissed Ithocles' corpse and then said, "Crack, crack! My heartstrings break, and my heart is broken.

"The prince of Argos is now Sparta's king."

"Command the singers who wait at the altar now to sing the fitting song I chose for my end."

Nearchus ordered, "Sirs, the song!"

All the singers sang:

"Glories, pleasures, pomps, delights, and ease
"Can please
"The outward senses only when the mind
"Is either untroubled or by peace refined."
The first singer sang:
"Crowns may flourish and decay,
"Beauties shine, but fade away."
The second singer sang:
"Youth may revel, yet it must
"Lie down in a bed of dust."
The third singer sang:
"Earthly honors flow and waste,
"Time alone does change and last."
All the singers sang:
"Sorrows mingled with contentments prepare
"Rest for care;
"Love only reigns in death; though art
"Can find no comfort for a broken heart."
As the singers stopped singing, Calantha died.

Armostes said, "Look to the queen!"

Bassanes said, "Her heart is broken, indeed. Oh, royal maiden, I wish that you had missed this act of your life! Yet it was a brave one. I must weep now that I see her smile in death."

Armostes said, "Wise Tecnicus! Thus said he:

"'When youth is ripe, and age from time does part,

"'The Lifeless Trunk shall wed the Broken Heart.'

"What he said is here fulfilled."

Nearchus said, "I am your king."

The other living people present said, "Long live Nearchus, King of Sparta!"

Nearchus said, "Calantha's last will shall never be digressed from. Wait in order upon these faithful lovers, as becomes us.

"The secret purposes of the gods are never known until men can call the consequences of them their own."

Appendix A: About the Author

It was a dark and stormy night. Suddenly a cry rang out, and on a hot summer night in 1954, Josephine, wife of Carl Bruce, gave birth to a boy — me. Unfortunately, this young married couple allowed Reuben Saturday, Josephine's brother, to name their first-born. Reuben, aka "The Joker," decided that Bruce was a nice name, so he decided to name me Bruce Bruce. I have gone by my middle name — David — ever since.

Being named Bruce David Bruce hasn't been all bad. Bank tellers remember me very quickly, so I don't often have to show an ID. It can be fun in charades, also. When I was a counselor as a teenager at Camp Echoing Hills in Warsaw, Ohio, a fellow counselor gave the signs for "sounds like" and "two words," then she pointed to a bruise on her leg twice. Bruise Bruise? Oh yeah, Bruce Bruce is the answer!

Uncle Reuben, by the way, gave me a haircut when I was in kindergarten. He cut my hair short and shaved a small bald spot on the back of my head. My mother wouldn't let me go to school until the bald spot grew out again.

Of all my brothers and sisters (six in all), I am the only transplant to Athens, Ohio. I was born in Newark, Ohio, and have lived all around Southeastern Ohio. However, I moved to Athens to go to Ohio University and have never left.

At Ohio U, I never could make up my mind whether to major in English or Philosophy, so I got a bachelor's degree with a double major in both areas, then I added a Master of Arts degree in English and a Master of Arts degree in Philosophy. Yes, I have my MAMA degree.

Currently, and for a long time to come (I eat fruits and veggies), I am spending my retirement writing books such as *Nadia Comaneci: Perfect 10*, *The Funniest People in Dance*, *Homer's* Iliad: *A Retelling in Prose*, and *William Shakespeare's* Othello: *A Retelling in Prose*.

By the way, my sister Brenda Kennedy writes romances such as *A New Beginning* and *Shattered Dreams*.

Appendix B: Some Books by David Bruce

Retellings of a Classic Work of Literature

Arden of Faversham*: A Retelling*

Ben Jonson's The Alchemist: *A Retelling*

Ben Jonson's The Arraignment, or Poetaster: *A Retelling*

Ben Jonson's Bartholomew Fair: *A Retelling*

Ben Jonson's The Case is Altered: *A Retelling*

Ben Jonson's Catiline's Conspiracy: *A Retelling*

Ben Jonson's The Devil is an Ass: *A Retelling*

Ben Jonson's Epicene: *A Retelling*

Ben Jonson's Every Man in His Humor: *A Retelling*

Ben Jonson's Every Man Out of His Humor: *A Retelling*

Ben Jonson's The Fountain of Self-Love, or Cynthia's Revels: *A Retelling*

Ben Jonson's The Magnetic Lady, or Humors Reconciled: *A Retelling*

Ben Jonson's The New Inn, or The Light Heart: *A Retelling*

Ben Jonson's Sejanus' Fall: *A Retelling*

Ben Jonson's The Staple of News: *A Retelling*

Ben Jonson's A Tale of a Tub: *A Retelling*

Ben Jonson's Volpone, or the Fox: *A Retelling*

Christopher Marlowe's Complete Plays: Retellings

Christopher Marlowe's Dido, Queen of Carthage: *A Retelling*

Christopher Marlowe's Doctor Faustus: *Retellings of the 1604 A-Text and of the 1616 B-Text*

Christopher Marlowe's Edward II: *A Retelling*

Christopher Marlowe's The Massacre at Paris: *A Retelling*

Christopher Marlowe's The Rich Jew of Malta: *A Retelling*

Christopher Marlowe's Tamburlaine, Parts 1 and 2: *Retellings*

Dante's Divine Comedy: *A Retelling in Prose*

Dante's Inferno: *A Retelling in Prose*

Dante's Purgatory: *A Retelling in Prose*

Dante's Paradise: *A Retelling in Prose*

The Famous Victories of Henry V: *A Retelling*

From the Iliad *to the* Odyssey: *A Retelling in Prose of Quintus of Smyrna's* Posthomerica

George Chapman, Ben Jonson, and John Marston's Eastward Ho! *A Retelling*

George Peele's The Arraignment of Paris: *A Retelling*

George Peele's The Battle of Alcazar: *A Retelling*

George Peele's David and Bathsheba, and the Tragedy of Absalom: *A Retelling*

George Peele's Edward I: *A Retelling*

George Peele's The Old Wives' Tale: *A Retelling*

George-a-Greene: *A Retelling*

The History of King Leir: *A Retelling*

Homer's Iliad: *A Retelling in Prose*

Homer's Odyssey: *A Retelling in Prose*

J.W. Gent.'s The Valiant Scot: *A Retelling*

Jason and the Argonauts: A Retelling in Prose of Apollonius of Rhodes' Argonautica

John Ford: Eight Plays Translated into Modern English

John Ford's The Broken Heart: *A Retelling*

John Ford's The Fancies, Chaste and Noble: *A Retelling*

John Ford's The Lady's Trial: *A Retelling*

John Ford's The Lover's Melancholy: *A Retelling*

John Ford's Love's Sacrifice: *A Retelling*

John Ford's Perkin Warbeck: *A Retelling*

John Ford's The Queen: *A Retelling*

John Ford's 'Tis Pity She's a Whore: *A Retelling*

John Lyly's Campaspe: *A Retelling*

John Lyly's Endymion, The Man in the Moon: *A Retelling*

John Lyly's Galatea: *A Retelling*

John Lyly's Love's Metamorphosis: *A Retelling*

John Lyly's Midas: *A Retelling*

John Lyly's Mother Bombie: *A Retelling*

John Lyly's Sappho and Phao: *A Retelling*

John Lyly's The Woman in the Moon: *A Retelling*

John Webster's The White Devil: *A Retelling*

King Edward III: *A Retelling*

Mankind: *A Medieval Morality Play* (A Retelling)

Margaret Cavendish's The Unnatural Tragedy: *A Retelling*

The Merry Devil of Edmonton: *A Retelling*

The Summoning of Everyman: *A Medieval Morality Play* (A Retelling)

Robert Greene's Friar Bacon and Friar Bungay: *A Retelling*

The Taming of a Shrew: *A Retelling*

Tarlton's Jests: A Retelling

Thomas Middleton's A Chaste Maid in Cheapside: *A Retelling*

Thomas Middleton's Women Beware Women: *A Retelling*

Thomas Middleton and Thomas Dekker's The Roaring Girl: *A Retelling*

Thomas Middleton and William Rowley's The Changeling: *A Retelling*

The Trojan War and Its Aftermath: Four Ancient Epic Poems

Virgil's Aeneid: *A Retelling in Prose*

William Shakespeare's 5 Late Romances: Retellings in Prose

William Shakespeare's 10 Histories: Retellings in Prose

William Shakespeare's 11 Tragedies: Retellings in Prose

William Shakespeare's 12 Comedies: Retellings in Prose

William Shakespeare's 38 Plays: Retellings in Prose

William Shakespeare's 1 Henry IV, aka Henry IV, Part 1: *A Retelling in Prose*

William Shakespeare's 2 Henry IV, aka Henry IV, Part 2: *A Retelling in Prose*

William Shakespeare's 1 Henry VI, aka Henry VI, Part 1: *A Retelling in Prose*

William Shakespeare's 2 Henry VI, aka Henry VI, Part 2: *A Retelling in Prose*

William Shakespeare's 3 Henry VI, aka Henry VI, Part 3: *A Retelling in Prose*

William Shakespeare's All's Well that Ends Well: *A Retelling in Prose*

William Shakespeare's Antony and Cleopatra: *A Retelling in Prose*

William Shakespeare's As You Like It: *A Retelling in Prose*

William Shakespeare's The Comedy of Errors: *A Retelling in Prose*

William Shakespeare's Coriolanus: *A Retelling in Prose*

William Shakespeare's Cymbeline: *A Retelling in Prose*

William Shakespeare's Hamlet: *A Retelling in Prose*

William Shakespeare's Henry V: *A Retelling in Prose*

William Shakespeare's Henry VIII: *A Retelling in Prose*

William Shakespeare's Julius Caesar: *A Retelling in Prose*

William Shakespeare's King John: *A Retelling in Prose*

William Shakespeare's King Lear: *A Retelling in Prose*

William Shakespeare's Love's Labor's Lost: *A Retelling in Prose*

William Shakespeare's Macbeth: *A Retelling in Prose*

William Shakespeare's Measure for Measure: *A Retelling in Prose*

William Shakespeare's The Merchant of Venice: *A Retelling in Prose*

William Shakespeare's The Merry Wives of Windsor: *A Retelling in Prose*

William Shakespeare's A Midsummer Night's Dream: *A Retelling in Prose*

William Shakespeare's Much Ado About Nothing: *A Retelling in Prose*

William Shakespeare's Othello: *A Retelling in Prose*

William Shakespeare's Pericles, Prince of Tyre: *A Retelling in Prose*

William Shakespeare's Richard II: *A Retelling in Prose*

William Shakespeare's Richard III: *A Retelling in Prose*

William Shakespeare's Romeo and Juliet: *A Retelling in Prose*

William Shakespeare's The Taming of the Shrew: *A Retelling in Prose*

William Shakespeare's The Tempest: *A Retelling in Prose*

William Shakespeare's Timon of Athens: *A Retelling in Prose*

William Shakespeare's Titus Andronicus: *A Retelling in Prose*

William Shakespeare's Troilus and Cressida: *A Retelling in Prose*

William Shakespeare's Twelfth Night: *A Retelling in Prose*

William Shakespeare's The Two Gentlemen of Verona: *A Retelling in Prose*

William Shakespeare's The Two Noble Kinsmen: *A Retelling in Prose*

William Shakespeare's The Winter's Tale: *A Retelling in Prose*